CW00859184

Myths

Myths

The Fourth Age: Shadow Wars, Book III

David N. Pauly

Dedication

To my loving wife, Minh Ha, who made this possible, and my brother James, the first to believe.

Contents

Chapter One

Platonia

Huw Gilliand prepared to leave the gardens surrounding the Well of Life in the center of Platonia an hour before sunset. He was to meet his friends, Berwyn, Reginard, and Rolant, at Berwyn's inn, the Bull and Boar, for supper. The gardens grew all around him, flowers and more beds of flowers in a rough circle, surrounding the ancient well. The well was more spring than well, but it had been called a well for hundreds of years, as waters from deep within the earth rose up and over moss-covered stones set low upon the ground. Brilliant blue water of a hue unknown outside the gardens streamed to the surface, pouring over a low stone lip worn smooth by countless centuries and splashing into a pool twelve feet wide and twenty feet long before forming a narrow, deep channel that flowed to the southern end of the gardens. There it sluiced away under a small arch to form the Stream of Life, slowly winding its way to the southern end of Platonia, where it merged with the great river Beadle and flowed into the sea.

Huw gazed about the gardens, surveying the new young plants in their fresh beds, replacements for the luxuriant flower beds destroyed by the Vandal, as he was known. Recalling the crime, Huw remembered the Man who had penetrated the safety and security of Platonia, laying waste to several flower beds: flowers that grew nowhere else, as far as Huw knew. How this Man could have invaded Platonia and why he had destroyed these flower beds was unknown, as he had refused to answer any questions. The Gracies took him to the eastern edge of Platonia and placed him in a boat to give him to Frederick, Prince of Amadeus, for trial.

Huw, as chief acolyte of the gardens, had been in the boat as Gracie rowers pushed away from the shore. Suddenly the Man, who had been silent for three days, began repeating a mantra that sounded much like a Shardan prayer Huw had heard once during his education with the Elves of Phoenicia. The boat was surrounded by water spirits, creatures that took corporeal form by amalgamating river foam, from which their name, Bubblers, was derived. They tipped the boat on its side and pulled the Vandal into the cold, swift-flowing water of the Beadle. He did not surface. As the rowers brought the boat back to the Platonia shore, Huw had been uneasy in his mind: such devotion to the destruction of a few plants made no logical sense to Huw.

A pacific people, the Gracies were shocked by this murder by their protectors, miscreant or no. Recalling the story brought sadness to Huw, though it was nearly a year since the incident. He was about to turn and leave the gardens, when he heard the unmistakable sounds of a Bubbler rising to the surface. Turning, he saw a bearded head form on the surface of the water, its translucent arms appearing and disappearing as the water fought to stay above its own surface in an endless dance.

'Huw, come to me now and listen,' said the Bubbler in a high-pitched voice, like that of a child making noises under water.

Shocked, Huw moved toward the Well; no living Gracie had ever heard a Bubbler speak outside the river Beadle, and even then, they offered greetings, not conversation. Striding back to the edge of the pool, Huw knelt and offered the traditional obeisance of an acolyte. Swiftly the Bubbler said, 'Platonia is in danger. We Bubblers are reaching the last of our strength.'

'You can't fail,' said a shocked Huw. 'You are the Bubblers, immortal river creatures who have always protected Platonia.'

'We are immortal, but if we cannot renew ourselves here in the Well of Life, we will become no more, and this we can no longer do.'

'Why not?'

'There is no time to explain; you must aid our renewal, or we will be lost, unable to protect Platonia against the greed of Men and the other races.'

'What can we do?' asked a stunned Huw.

'You must save the Gemwings, our only source of hope, or we will disappear in less than a year.'

'Gemwings,' asked Huw, thinking of the legendary insects, presumed to exist, but never actually seen. 'How can I save the Gemwings? Do they even exist?'

'You will come to know that from the Gemwings themselves. Only they can tell you how to save them, us, and Platonia. Fail and you doom Platonia to the destruction of Men.' With that the Bubbler dissolved back into the waters of the well.

Rising, Huw moved woodenly toward the entrance of the gardens, in shock from the conversation. Simple wooden doors were there, ritually closed at sunset and opened at dawn, when the acolytes would gather around the Well of Life, dipping into its unique waters and feeling the life force of Nostraterra course through their bodies.

Becoming an acolyte was a choice made by Gracies at any time of their lives, but their desire had to be granted by the Bubblers. Gracies wanting to serve the Bubblers would immerse themselves in the icy waters of the Beadle each spring equinox. Those chosen by the Bubblers were touched on the shoulder by a Bubbler, but those rejected would have only minutes of life before the icy cold waters leached the heat from their bones.

If you served as an acolyte you were respected greatly, and you could drink the Waters of Life every day; an excess usually frowned upon by Gracies. The Waters of Life extended a Gracie's lifespan from the usual hundred years or so to nearly two hundred years.

Now Huw, chief acolyte during his time, had the impossible task of securing the safety of Platonia by saving the legendary Gemwings. Every midsummer's night, the gardens were closed and all were forbidden from entering, even if their need was compelling. During the dark of the moon, when only the stars shone down, the acolytes listened for the high-pitched buzzing of many wings, which according to history signaled the arrival of the Gemwings into the gardens. Once an ambitious Gracie hid within the gardens to see the mythical Gemwings, but all heard a terrible shriek within the gardens and all nearby felt a dark foreboding and dared not enter the gardens that night. The next day, no trace of the Gracie was found; only later, along the shores of the southern end of Platonia, were his clothes found.

The Gemwings were a mysterious implacable force to be reckoned with; their secrets were their own, undisclosed even by the Bubblers. Huw shook his head when he thought that he was charged to seek out the creatures of myth and legend, much less make contact with them. Leaving the gardens, he closed the doors behind him and strode off, shaking and trembling in fear, toward Berwyn's inn to have dinner with his friends.

Huw paused on a simple country lane covered in white gravel as evening drew down upon him, fifty feet or so from the Bull and Boar, unsure of what to say to his friends, with little idea as to how to find the Gemwings, much less save them. Approaching the inn, he smelled the delicious nutty odor of fresh-baked bread, roasted potatoes, and the somewhat disquieting aroma of roasting meats. Huw, while abstaining from meat of any kind, did not criticize those who consumed it, but the thought of eating something that had once drawn breath made him shudder.

Striding forward, Huw entered the inn and saw the usual crowd of Gracies come in from their farms and orchards. Late spring meant many of the folk were exercising their elbows after finishing the last of the planting or pruning. Hearing his name called from across the room, Huw saw his friends, Berwyn, Rolly, and Reggie, gathered at a far table in the corner away from the fire. Huw tried to force the fear and uncertainty of the Bubbler's news from his mind as he ordered another full pitcher of ale from a Gracie server, then joined his friends with false cheer, hoping to enjoy 'an ale and a tale,' as Berwyn said.

Berwyn, his oldest friend, glanced up at him and, seeing the poorly hidden concern, asked, 'Huw, are you alright?'

'Fine, fine,' said Huw in a slightly breathless voice. 'I see that business is good.'

'No worse than usual,' replied Berwyn dourly. 'You are just in time to hear the tale of Reggie and Rolly now that they have returned from their camping trip.'

'Camping trip, yes, I forgot for a moment—you've been gone over a week. Where did you go?' asked Huw in a thin voice.

'We were on the Flowery Plateau,' began Rolly, when Reggie hushed him and said, 'Let's not be overheard.'

Huw knew that the flowery plateau was formed by the divergence of the river Beadle at the north end of Platonia and encompassed nearly a hundred square miles of wild flowers and grasses. A dense barrier of trees over a mile wide divided the farms and grazing pastures of the Gracies from the plateau, which was best reached by boat rather than through the tangled forest.

Huw received another concerned look from Berwyn, but ignoring it said, 'Overheard? What are you talking about?'

Rolly said, 'I don't want people laughing at me again.'

'Laughing about what?' asked Huw.

Rolly's ears began to flush when Berwyn, the least imaginative of the group, said, 'Oh you're not on about that giant dragonfly again, are you? On the Plateau? One of the mythical Gemwings?'

'Yes,' replied Rolly heatedly. 'And if you want to know, it was to get another glimpse of a Gemwing that Reggie and I spent a week camping and quietly walking around the plateau.'

'Enough. Let's adjourn to the roof before we continue this conversation.' said Huw. Taking their tankards of ale with them, each of the Gracies grabbed a fresh pitcher from the bar and then followed Berwyn up the inner stair to the wooden deck surrounded by a wooden lattice fence, where several tables and chair stood. Tonight it was a bit cool, and they had the deck to themselves.

'Now lock the door,' demanded Huw of Berwyn.

His friend moved to do so, muttering under his breath.

'What do you mean *another*?' asked Huw. 'When did you see one the first time?'

'I saw one last month, or at least I think so, from one of my family's ferry boats that I used to fish above the landing,' said Rolly defensively. 'It was a Gemwing, I tell you.'

'A Gemwing, are you certain?' asked Huw with a leap in his heart.

'Well, the spring floods haven't started yet with the cold weather, and the usual ferry traffic slowed down the past weeks, so I had time to see if there was really a Gemwing up on the Flowery Plateau. Reggie wanted to come along, and we just got back.'

'You could have been killed, both of you! You know what happened to the last Gracie that was caught by the Gemwings, don't you?' demanded a flustered Berwyn.

'Of course we know! But that Gracie just disappeared, didn't he?' retorted Rolly. 'No one knows what actually happened to him. Besides, chasing myths makes a welcome break from work.'

'And did you see one?' asked Huw.

'No,' said Rolly.

'There, I told you,' began Berwyn with a look of smug satisfaction.

'It was Reggie who saw the Gemwing this time,' said Rolly. 'Go on, Reggie, tell them.'

Sheepishly, Reggie said, 'It was late in the evening three nights ago. We had finished our meal and had some ale from our packs, but I couldn't sleep, so I got up and walked away from the fire a few yards and saw the full moon just begin to rise in the east. I listened to the water in the river for a few minutes and began to get sleepy, so I turned back toward the fire. Suddenly the tip of my nose was burnt, and I saw a flash of color and giant wings disappearing into the night.'

This elicited a dark laugh from Berwyn. 'Serves you right for drinking and walking in your sleep; lucky you didn't fall in the river instead.'

'Ignore him, Reggie,' said Huw. 'What happened next?'

'Nothing,' said Rolly. 'I put some salve on my nose and lay down to sleep.'

'So you think that was a Gemwing?' asked Berwyn dubiously, ignoring Huw's glance to keep silent.

'Yes,' replied Reggie mulishly. 'How do you get your nose burnt from cool, damp air when you are a dozen feet from a campfire banked in its own ashes?'

'Huw, help me here,' implored Berwyn. 'You spent years amongst the Elves and are the chief acolyte of the Gardens. Did you ever hear of anything more outlandish than this tale?'

'Yes, as a matter of fact. Today I spoke with a Bubbler.'

Briefly Huw explained his encounter with the Bubbler in the Garden. Seeing even Berwyn's skeptical face go pale, he finished his tale by stating that he had to go in search of the mythical Gemwings.

'How are we supposed to find a mystical beast that doesn't want to be found, much less help it in some way?' asked Berwyn. 'Wait—you've never treated us as fools despite your education. You're not starting now, are you?'

'No,' insisted a still shaken Huw, though the strong ale he was gulping was helping steady his nerves a bit. 'A Bubbler has never spoken to a Gracie outside the river. Either the Bubblers have gone mad or we are in real trouble.'

'Trouble, how are we in trouble?' asked an astounded Berwyn.

'Weren't you listening?' demanded Reggie, who had gone white as a sheet. 'As go the Bubblers, so goes Platonia, or so say the legends. My father has reports of groups of brigands roaming up and down the east bank of the Beadle, looking for a way to cross into Platonia.'

Reggie's father, Ifan Colchester, was the First Speaker of Platonia, and amongst his many duties was the security of Platonia, which involved keeping the other races out.

'The Mayor of Alton sent a message warning of groups of brigands coming through town causing mischief, stealing food, trying to steal tools and horses. There was a small fight, and three brigands were killed, along with a sheriff of Alton, before they were driven off. But the Mayor fears they will be back sooner rather than later. He has sent to Amadeus, asking the prince for his help in sending these violent layabouts packing, but his messenger has not returned yet. Regardless, we are on our own for now, and if the Bubblers disappear or lose their powers, then nothing will stand in the way of an invasion of Platonia.'

Huw knew that Alton was the only town outside Platonia where Gracies were welcome and freely traded with the other races without fear of persecution.

'Invasion? End of the Bubblers?' sputtered Berwyn. 'Huw, you and Reggie seem to have lost your wits! Do you believe this nonsense, Rolly?'

'I saw a Gemwing last year,' said Rolly. 'Reggie got his nose burnt somehow, and, no, we didn't drink enough ale for him to imagine his story. If Huw says that the Bubblers are dying and need to be saved somehow, I believe him. Reggie's story about Men encroaching makes sense. My ferryman reported Men trying to negotiate passage into Platonia at a very high price, but they are always refused, according to our law. Also, several boats of Men, or what was left of them, were recently found in the great swirl that exists where the rivers of the Beadle come together again south of Platonia. Clearly, Platonia is in danger, and maybe, as Huw says, finding the Gemwings could help.'

All Gracies knew the characteristics of Men, a race that embraced the wholesale destruction of woods and wild meadows, and slew beasts for sport. No Men had ever been allowed into Platonia, and none ever would be.

'Regardless,' said Huw with false cheerfulness, 'if the Bubblers were simply telling me a cautionary tale, or if this one Bubbler was mad, we can all use a break from our routine.' He had recovered much of his composure, thanks to the effect of the ale upon his nerves. 'Let's plan getting away for a week, and this time we can cover the entire Plateau with horses.'

'While you are my good friend, and I will help if I can, remind me again why I want to come along?' asked a confused and frustrated Berwyn. 'I have a new batch of beer to brew and accounts to be overseen that will take me at least the next two weeks.'

'Fine,' replied Huw. 'You stay here and run the tavern and see what sort of adventures you will miss by not being with us. Remember the time you didn't go with me to visit the Dwarves?'

Grumpily, Berwyn remembered that day. He had thought that Huw was just going to walk for a short while with a traveling company of Dwarves from the Ocean Range, but the Dwarves had invited his friend to a feast in their mines, and Huw had been gone for two weeks. When he returned, he had stories to tell for months about the Dwarves, their customs, language, and, worst of all, their remarkable ale. Berwyn would have given his eyeteeth for a chance to sample this most mysterious ale and try to cadge a few tricks of its making from the Dwarves. Instead, he had been too busy running his tavern to go with Huw. That had been last fall, and he had rarely regretted anything more than that misstep.

'Alright, alright, I will go with you,' said Berwyn. 'Let me just tell my brother that I will be away for a week or so. When do you want to go?'

'Well, we need to leave as soon as possible,' replied Huw. 'We must be ready to depart at midday tomorrow. It will be full moon in two nights, which should help us find the Gemwings as reputedly they only fly at night.'

'How are we supposed to help the Gemwings? What are we supposed to do?' persisted Berwyn. 'The Dwarves I understand, but dragonflies?'

'You didn't understand the Dwarves at the time, and look what happened,' replied Huw. 'Now we must keep the purpose of our trip secret, for if the Brigands learn all of this, they might try to interfere. After all, if the Gemwings really do exist, and we fail to help them, the Bubblers will die, and without their protection, the Brigands will be free to attack Platonia. Besides, we do not want to panic the Gracies into thinking our protectors are dying.'

To this they all agreed. Huw descended the stairs and, leaving coins enough to pay for their ale, went home to consult his father and the books of lore that they kept. Reggie and Rolly also left to organize gear and horses for a week's camping expedition.

Berwyn descended the stairs to find his older brother, Glynn. Outwardly pragmatic, Berwyn reflected the dour personality of his father, Largo Loudberry, when it came to life in general, but inwardly he thought that life in Platonia was too tame and dreamed of someday journeying to the lands of legend, Kozak and Eldora, and maybe even meeting an Elf in his travels.

Walking over to Glynn, a non-descript Gracie, graying at the temples, who stood behind the main bar, he said, 'Can you run the inn for a week or so? Rolly, Reggie, Huw, and I are going to Alton to look for new business opportunities.'

'It's a good idea,' said Glynn. 'Right, you go and have a look see and let me know what you find.'

* * *

The next morning, Berwyn woke at his customary dawn hour. Glancing out the window of his small room above the inn, he saw the early gray light was streaked with pink in the east. It promised to be a fair day, with no rain. Dressing quickly in loose clothes made for riding, he went downstairs and saw that the bakers were already hard at work. Today they were mostly making rye bread, with a few sweetened buns for breakfast.

Berwyn then went to the malting sheds, where the barley was being spread over the malting tables. Shallow trestle trays held the barley as just a little water was added to begin the process of changing the barley from grain into the precursor of beer. Too little water, and the resulting wort was thin and bitter; too much water, and the barley would mold.

It was an exacting task, but few in Platonia malted their barley as well as the Loudberrys. Berwyn's family had long ago perfected an excellent smooth brown ale, not too bitter with hops, nor too sweet; it had a rich, nutty flavor that lingered in the mouth and on the tongue.

In late summer, the beer that had made the inn famous was brewed with fresh fruits of different kinds, making it almost more like wine than beer. The recipe was a closely guarded secret, and Berwyn stockpiled wheat all year long so no one would know that the recipe called for half lightly malted barley and half malted wheat. Berwyn's father discovered malted wheat by accident one day when some wheat had mistakenly been mixed into the barley in a trestle tray. Not wanting to waste the grain, Largo had tried malting it to see what would happen, and the resulting beer was truly unspectacular: pale and mildly flavored.

But then serendipity intervened. Young Glynn had been eating raspberries, and, when his father had left the kitchen, added some to the beer. Returning, Largo had absently sipped the beer and made a peculiar face as the flavor of the fruit had made its presence known. Looking into the bottom of the mug, he saw the raspberries. But instead of being angry, he threw back his head and laughed. It took several barrels before he got the measures right, trying different fruits before he found the right mix of flavors. Now all of Platonia looked forward to the end of harvest, when raspberries, peaches, and blackberries were all made into their individual beers, commanding twice the price of regular beer.

Lately, the Gracie folk of Alton had heard of this beer, and there was demand to ship it abroad. Berwyn and Glynn had talked about expanding the beer-making portion of the inn and creating an actual independent brewery. Huw had offered the investment money, and Berwyn planned to start building the new brewery once he returned from this trip. While it might be a waste of time, there might be some wild strains of barley or other grains on the Plateau that could be cultivated and used to enhance their beer.

Packing saddle bags for his horses, he made certain to bring rain gear, heavy cloaks, and sweaters in case the weather turned inclement, and, most importantly, food. Erring on the side of caution, Berwyn packed three weeks' worth of dried and preserved staples, including several jars of preserved mushrooms, a stout keg of ale, and even several cases of Bullsblood wine, mature and hale. Seeing the horses' packs were properly laden and ready, he returned to the inn.

* * *

Huw walked to the inn, knowing that Berwyn had a horse for him. His youthful face was drawn and haggard from a late night studying the lore books with his father; only as dawn broke had he fallen asleep for a few hours. But all he and his father had found was an ancient whistle given to Huw by Alfredus, Lord of Phoenicia, when he had departed Phoenicia two years ago, along with a vague hint from his Elven teachers that it might come in handy someday.

Arriving at the inn, he took a seat in the common room to wait for Reggie and Rolly. Glynn brought him a breakfast of eggs and fried potatoes, toast, and a jug of rich coffee.

Huw was next in line for the hereditary title of Lord of the Manor of Thackery, a village whose confines were five by seven miles, but Huw was more concerned about learning than inheriting wealth. Seven years ago, his father had sent him to study with the Greater Elves of Phoenicia, keeping alive the family tradition of education so there would always be someone who could not only read the histories of the Gracies but speak and read the ancient languages of all the races. Every generation, the Gilliand family sent someone to study with the Elves, and Huw had spent five years there before returning to Platonia two years ago. Huw had come back from Phoenicia seemingly a little older than his years would lead people to believe, and he rarely spoke of his time there outside of his family. Few Gracies thought academic study a worthwhile pursuit, content to lead a rustic, uneducated life, and Huw was content for the most part to keep his education to himself, although after too much ale he had been known to recite Elvish poetry at the Bull and Boar.

Huw looked up as Berwyn returned and, signaling his brother for a plate of breakfast, joined Huw in a cup of coffee.

'Well, Berwyn, are you ready for an adventure?' asked Huw tiredly.

'The Plateau in late spring—not quite climbing the Never Summer Range is it?' he replied.

'Perhaps, perhaps not,' replied Huw, 'but if the Gemwings are real and they need our help, who knows where we might go and what we might have to do?'

Reggie and Rolly arrived together and, having breakfasted already, sat to enjoy a cup of coffee.

'Reggie and I are ready,' announced Rolly. 'If we leave before noon, we should have enough time to make it to the village of Toadhollow if we push the horses fairly hard, and we can spend the night there. We should make the docks late the next afternoon, and we can load the boats to go north.'

'Boats?' said Berwyn. 'Nobody said anything about boats. You all know I hate boats.'

Snorting, Rolly replied, 'You get sick when your horse gallops, so I am not looking forward to being on a boat with you, either, but how else do you expect to go up the river quietly? Besides, it's the best way to see where to start. The Plateau is quite dense with shrubs and trees up there. It's hard to find anything even if you trip over it—probably why the Gemwing likes it up there, come to think of it.'

Rolly's father had inherited the family's ferry business, and Rolly was in charge of managing the fleet of boats that went up and down the Beadle, while Rolly's uncle—Reggie's father—was in charge of the family messenger business. The Colchesters could not have competed against Men and their messengers, much less their trade boats, but the river was impossible for Men to cross. Eldoran law prohibited their entry into Platonia, and geography was another barrier. North of Platonia the river was impassable; cataracts and rapids, steep cliffs and dense forests comprised the upper banks of the Beadle. Southward, the river briefly grew wider and flatter before it passed through the impenetrable expanse of the Dark Forest, becoming a narrow, fierce course of water running along the southwest highlands. Men could either ride around south of the Dark Forest, ferrying the river with their news or goods, or use a Gracie or Dwarf as a messenger or merchant. Few Dwarves, other than the occasional messenger Dwarf, regularly passed through Platonia, so the Colchesters had a business for which there was an ever-increasing demand and no real competition.

* * *

An hour later, the four young Gracies were mounted on their horses and proceeding eastward along the main road that bisected Platonia east and west, the spring sun warm on their backs as a soft southern breeze brought the smell of a nearby apple orchard wafting over them. Afternoon shadows were lengthening in front of them when they finally stopped for lunch on the side of the road. Several Gracies greeted them in passing, but Huw was too preoccupied with the warnings of the Bubbler to do more than nod to other travelers. Remounting their horses, they slowed their cantering to a brisk walk followed by a trot, as even Reggie grew weary of the pace that they had set for themselves. They saw the village of Toadhollow before them as the sun was dipping below the horizon, and they gently urged their horses ahead. Sensing the end of their day's journey, the horses willingly complied, and within the hour the travelers found themselves in the stable yard of the Leaping Frog Inn.

That night they enjoyed good plain food. The inn was famous for its beer and for its pies, preserved in winter and fresh in late summer and early fall. Shown to a private dining room to eat, the Gracies tucked into their food, and half an hour later they pushed back from the table with a sigh. Returning to the common room, they spoke with other Gracies and swapped heard stories and rumors with one another.

One of the more interesting tales came from a Border Guard, a distant relation to the Wiltstones who was newly come from Wiltland, where he had seen the First Speaker. 'Men,' he said, 'are cutting down the trees just across the river from us, setting up farms just outside our lands, more and more of them each month.'

'Besides our river guardians, I thought the laws of Eldora precluded Men from entering Platonia,' said Berwyn.

'They do,' said Huw. 'Eldora's Edict of Sanctuary declared Platonia a free land immediately after the Great War. Their King Ladarion placed Platonia under the protection of the northern scepter of the princedom of Amadeus. No man may enter Platonia under this law.'

'Nor have they,' said the border guard. 'But they are too close for my peace of mind. I told the First Speaker the same thing.'

'What did he say?' asked Huw.

'He said that for now the rivers keep Men out of our lands, but if they can get around the Bubblers someday, there will be trouble—trouble like we haven't seen.'

After a few more rounds of drinks and stories, Huw and the others climbed the stairs to their room, a comfortable chamber with four soft beds. The Gracies were asleep in minutes, except for Huw, who tossed and turned, thinking about what lay ahead and what was going on along the borders of Platonia.

The next morning they were up shortly after dawn. After a quick breakfast they mounted their horses and headed for the ferries at East Point. Reggie and Rolly chatted away in the saddle, and even Berwyn actively participated in the conversation, but Huw was preoccupied with their mission to find the Gemwings and the renewal of the Bubblers. Truth be told, the Gracies needed protection. Their history clearly demonstrated that they could not survive amongst the other races.

The Gracies had come from within the lands of Men from all over Nostraterra. A millennium ago, a great plague had swept Nostraterra, slaying multitudes of Men but not affecting Dwarves or Elves. The victims of this plague had turned blue, gasping for air as their lungs filled with a foul fluid. No healing herb or potion was found that would stem this disease once contracted. The plague spread in distinct pockets: some regions of Men were unaffected, while others were decimated. Rumors were rife. Some Men spoke of a terrible large-winged creature that had been seen shortly before the arrival of plague. Others blamed a mysterious blue-haired woman whose beautiful features were a mix of Elf and Man.

Whatever the origin of the plague, after seven years of terror and death, the sickness consumed itself, and no new plague victims had been seen since. Of those infected, few survived ... and while the plague did not mark the survivors with any outward sign, it had left a mark upon them.

Every child of a survivor was born small and slender and grew to be far smaller in height and stature than their parents. These plague children, as they came to be known, preferred the company of other children with their condition, and in any case were quickly isolated by their communities.

From Eldora to Kozak, from the Hermits of the southwest highlands to the men of Chilton, these plague children were born and flourished within the confines of their physique. As they grew to adulthood, many were abused or otherwise taken advantage of by Men, who were stronger and tougher than they were. The Gracies, as they were called after their obsequious, placating manners, learned to be stealthy, moving without being seen or heard. They banded together and came to the conclusion that they could not live in harmony with Men. Nor could they go to the Dwarves, though they were closer in height to Dwarves than to Men. But the Dwarves welcomed them no more than Men did, and as for the Elves, both Greater and Lesser, they, too, shunned the plague children.

Hunted and persecuted, the Gracies created a silent speech of hand gestures unintelligible to the other races. These hand signals were still used today, allowing Gracies private communications with one another; every child was taught at least the rudiments of these signals as soon as they could talk. Peaceful by nature, they refused to fight, trying to simply farm and trade with Men and the other races, but the aggressive, exploitive nature of Men caused them to be hunted and chased from their lands. Only after a last, desperate flight, in which they had stayed just days ahead of murderous bands of criminal looters, did they find Platonia.

The Bubblers found them to be the perfect inhabitants of an unsullied land uninhabited for millennia, called Platonia. Platonia had been protected by the river spirits against all sentient intruders, but now, rather than keeping the Gracies out of the land, the river spirits gave them permission to settle there and promised to protect them as long as they protected the land. Within their new realm, the Gracies flourished, content with their isolation, living at one with the land and laboring hard to care for their beautiful gift.

Rolly's voice broke in upon Huw's thoughts. 'Why so quiet, Huw? It's a beautiful spring day, and my father will give us quite a feast on our arrival. Don't fret! We will find these Gemwings somehow, and we will be back home as soon as we help them.'

'I hope you are right,' said Huw. 'But the uncertainty of finding them, much less knowing how to help them, has me worried. Sorry, lads, I will try to be more cheerful.'

Gradually Huw began to participate in the conversation, but a corner of his mind remained focused on their mission. At last they arrived at Rolly's ancestral family home, Flowstone, and Rolly's father, Marmaduke, laid on quite a feast for his son and his guests. Swaying from the wine and food, the four young Gracies crawled into bed shortly after midnight.

Early the next morning, the Gracies descended the stairs to the breakfast table with aching heads. None of them had much of an appetite, though they gladly drank the strong Shardan coffee Marmaduke had ordered his cook to prepare.

Blearily they mounted their horses for the short ride to the east Ferry, where trade goods were off-loaded on the east side of the Beadle. Here there were warehouses, a small set of shops, and an inn. Men who wanted their messages taken to the far side of Platonia reported to Rolly's messenger business. Sure enough, as the building drew into sight, an express pony could be seen galloping west into Platonia, carrying a message for the merchants of Alton, or for Men who wished to trade either with Gracies or the Dwarves of the Ocean Range. Much trade was conducted throughout Platonia, and the Gracie Council, a group of elders chosen by the adult populace every ten years, had wisely kept customs duties so low that there was no point in trying to take goods the long way around.

Approaching the docks, the Gracies saw that Rolly had ordered a messenger boat prepared, with a flat carrier for the horses as well. Several Gracies were manning the boat and carrier.

'It was excellent planning to have our transport arranged,' Huw told Rolly. 'But what about keeping our journey quiet?'

'Well, I have included fishing gear along with our packs and staves,' answered Rolly with a wink. 'As far as anyone knows, we are on a holiday for a fortnight. So I told my lads, and so they will tell anyone who may ask. A messenger boat will ply the river up and down each day in case we are finished early, but I told them not to start for a week. Otherwise our story would be a bit thin. If after a week we are bored or haven't caught any fish, our return would be believable.'

The horses and gear were quickly stowed, and the Gracies found themselves comfortable seats and watched the boat crew efficiently erect the sails and cast off. The wind strongly blew from the southwest as it often did in late spring, and they steadily made good time against the current.

'When do you expect we shall arrive?' asked Huw.

'If this wind holds, we should be there in the morning; it is sixteen leagues north of here as the crow flies, but more as the river flows,' replied Rolly.

They began talking amongst themselves about common things in Platonia, and as the day drew on, the Gracies ate from provisions brought on board before their journey.

Watching the sun set behind a distant bank of clouds, Huw remarked, 'It looks like rain. With this moist wind, it would not surprise me if the weather turned tomorrow, just in time for us to start our trip.'

Rolly Reggie, and Berwyn enjoyed fresh river fish, but Huw kept to his vegetarian diet. Afterward, all but Huw and the boat crew turned in for the night.

Huw leaned over the side, reflecting on the waters gurgling alongside the barge's hull. The Beadle River descended from an enormous watershed from the Never Summer Range and had great vigor in its melt waters. Even in high summer, the river was too deep and too swift to ford on foot or horseback, and the ferry boats, using a rope tied to each bank, provided the only means available to cross the river. The river split into two branches as it encountered the north hills. One branch split east, the other west, forming a nearly perfect oval of land seventy miles wide and fifty miles long: Platonia. Clean ran the waters of the Beadle, and the Gracies made certain that no waste from their homes or farms drained into the river. Except at the two crossing points, the wild growth of Platonia, the ancient trees and marshes, grasslands and hillsides, were left alone for at least one mile in from the river on all sides.

Legend held the Bubblers to be the least known magical manifestations of Nostraterra, akin to the Water Spirits of the Elves. The Bubblers were able to sense the intent of any sentient creature along the river. Elves were generally allowed to pass, Lesser Elves without question. They could either swim or use their own boats. Few Elves, Greater or Lesser, would take the time to fight the swift current of the river northward and would instead journey on horseback and then take a Gracie boat into Platonia. Dwarves were also allowed free passage, under strict Gracie supervision, as the Bubblers sensed no evil inherent in them. But Men were a different matter. Bubblers had adopted the feelings of the Gracies against their ancient enemies and prevented any Men from crossing the river. Simple Men merchants trying to get their goods through Platonia were diverted by the Bubblers back to the far banks of the rivers. Sometimes, however, bands of brigands would attempt to breach the borders, and against such trespassers the Bubblers showed no pity or remorse. The boats would be driven onto rocks or sunken logs and the Men pulled to their deaths in the cold, pitiless depths of the river.

Huw did not appreciate violence in any form, and he wished that no one would ever die again trying to access Platonia. The Bubblers were still the key to preserving the life of the Gracies, however, and if the Bubblers were forced to use violence, there was nothing that Huw could do.

Now, as he stopped recalling ancient history, he found that he was finally sleepy. Turning in, he lay in a reasonably comfortable hammock, in a tiny cabin by himself. As he swayed gently, the murmuring of the river lulled him to sleep.

* * *

In the morning, the Gracies awoke to the sound of distant thunder and saw mist along the river. The trees grew closer now that they had left the farmlands far behind, and the sky was thick and gray with moisture.

'Fine day for an adventure,' remarked the boat captain. 'I don't relish your trip today. If my nose is right, it will rain for the better part of the afternoon and be cool and foggy for several days thereafter. Why not return to East Point with us and leave again in a few days' time?'

Huw, remembering the urgency of the Bubbler, said that they would make do and find ways to relax even in foul weather.

After three more hours, they reached the point where Rolly and Reggie had come ashore. The boat could proceed no farther, as the Beadle grew narrow and rapid, with an enormous rocky point, covered in trees almost to the water's edge, jutting into the flow. East of the point, the banks were only separated by forty feet, with a sharp high cliff on the eastern shore, with an enormous ash tree casting its branches across the river.

The landing point was little more than a small clearing on south side of the promontory, sheltered by the rapid current of the Beadle. Unloading the horses was difficult, and several of the Gracie deck hands got wet when they missed their footing, but within an hour or so all the horses were off and re-saddled, if bedraggled, and Huw and his friends were ready to depart.

The thunder was growing louder and nearer, and the captain cheerfully said, 'I will send the messenger boat sooner than we had planned, for Wiltstones are not known for staying out in the wet and cold!'

Muttering under his breath about impudent Colchesters, Reggie kept his peace as Rolly laughed and said, 'We shall return with new tales to tell, if not a cold. Farewell.'

The young Gracies led their horses single file. Rolly and Reggie were in front, followed by Huw and Berwyn. A cold rain began spitting from the skies, prompting the Gracies to don heavy cloaks, which would prove a poor respite from the rain as eventually water would soak through.

Huw stopped the others and, to their surprise, opened one of his packs and removed cloaks of heavy canvas.

'What are these?' asked Berwyn.

'Waterproof cloaks,' said Huw. 'I prepared them over the summer—the canvas is saturated in lard, then allowed to dry in the sun, then saturated again, and dried again, the process repeated many times. Last of all I added a coat of beeswax.'

'Where did you learn such a thing?' asked Reggie.

'I thought of it one day,' said Huw with a smile. 'There are enough for all of us—and for our mounts as well once we make camp.'

Soon a steady rain began to fall. Thunder rumbled and grumbled overhead, and gusts of wind bent the limbs of the trees. Yet thanks to the cloaks, the Gracies stayed relatively dry. Their horses whickered and muttered but stayed the course, their exercise keeping them warm.

As the day turned into afternoon, the Gracies paused under a large maple tree to have a cold nuncheon prepared by the boat crew. Drinking from ale flasks, they were all merrier when they resumed their journey.

Rolly was retracing his prior path, but seeing that they were looking for a dragonfly that seemed to come out only at night, they intended to ride farther north and skirt the beginnings of the great shrub lands and the vast meadows of wild flowers that grew in numbers uncounted upon the plateau. This seemed the most likely place to see the Gemwing if it existed, and to look for any barley or other unusual plants. Berwyn was not terribly sanguine about their chances, but even he had to admit it was a welcome change from running the inn.

The forest gradually thinned, and at last they reached the flowers and grasslands of the Plateau. The Gracies made camp under the encircling boughs of two ash trees and tended to their horses before themselves. As the horses contentedly munched their oat bags and swished their tails, the Gracies saw steam rising from the collar holes of their canvas cloaks placed on when they made camp.

'Capital idea,' said Reggie. 'Huw, I am quite impressed.'

'These are just trial cloaks. My father and I have not had a chance to really use them before. But now we can try them out in heavy weather, away from prying eyes that might poach on our ideas,' said Huw.

'You mean steal them, don't you?' asked Berwyn.

'Yes, here there is no one to see us,' said Huw.

Huw's idea to test these cloaks where no one could see had merit. Therefore, his friends did not complain as sheets of rain fell around them, while they sat outside their tents. After dinner and wine, the Gracies began to nod off, and presently Berwyn and Huw were the only ones awake, quietly chatting about the new brewery, before entering their tents to sleep.

The next morning, the Gracies woke to a sodden landscape of dark, dank trees shrouded in fog. The mist was so thick that little could be seen more than ten yards from their faces.

Taking Rolly's advice, the Gracies did not travel that day, using a long rope to venture from camp in search of firewood. The sodden wood on the ground was useless, but the dead limbs still on trees could be encouraged to burn with some cooking oil, and Rolly was able to rekindle their fire on his return to camp. The day passed slowly, as there are only so many new things you can think to say to your oldest friends.

Wrapped in silence, the Gracies were unaware of the time but suddenly realized they had dozed or talked right through lunch, and it was now time for dinner. Little happened during the night except the horses became nervous well after midnight; it took Berwyn arising from his blankets to quiet them again.

The next day dawned colder and clearer, with the wind blowing briskly from the northwest. Smaller clouds scudded by, with large patches of blue sky between them. The land was sodden but slowly reviving under a warm spring sun.

Laughing, for nothing ever seems as grim in the bright light of day as it does in the dark of night, Rolly said, 'Let that dragonfly hide from us now!'

Smiling, Huw said, 'Let us ride east along the tree line toward the river and then search westward through the shorter trees. This will give us the lay of the land, and we shall then think about how we shall find what is hidden in plain sight.'

The Gracies mounted their horses and started off at a brisk trot. Huw pulled the small silver whistle that the Elves had given him from an old leather pouch and blew into it. Two different tones sounded, one a buzzing sound that became quite annoying, and the other an extremely high-pitched sound that much of the time was inaudible to the Gracies. Seeing their quizzical looks, Huw said confidently, 'It's an ancient whistle.'

'Really, I thought it was a tiny little catapult that would throw a tiny net to catch a dragonfly,' remarked Berwyn, shaking his head. 'Of course it's a whistle, but why are you blowing it now? It's giving me a headache. And where did you get it, anyway?'

'I think it was the wine rather than the whistle,' said Rory.

Just as a quarrel was about to break out; Huw coughed importantly and said, 'I was given this by Alfredus when I studied in Phoenicia. He said that it might come in handy someday, and I can't think of a better day than today. Who knows, it might actually work.'

'Blow then if you must,' grumbled Berwyn, 'but ride ahead a bit so it's not so loud.'

Looking around them for the first half hour quickly became tedious. No matter how much Huw blew and no matter what sequence, nothing happened. Gratefully, they stopped for a quick lunch.

'At least you can't toot on that thing while your mouth is full of food,' remarked Rolly wryly.

Nearly choking on his food, Berwyn grinned at his best friend, and even Huw could not repress a smile, even though he was the only one who actually believed in the myths and legends completely.

All that day, no dragonflies did they see, but Berwyn found a wild sprig of barley that looked a little different from the plants that were used in Platonia. Marking the place for their return, the Gracies pressed on until they reached the river at mid-afternoon.

Turning around, they decided to have a brief snack back at their campsite and then press on westward until they could no longer see. Huw resumed his whistling, even louder, if truth be told, than before, atonal, irregular and shrill. Berwyn eventually begged Huw to be quiet, but Huw just went on playing, to the distraction and distress of the rest.

Little did they see that day besides a few startled deer and rabbits, too young to be shot for food. As the evening drew on, even Huw's spirits began to fall. They had seen nothing more interesting than Berwyn's barley all day, and the evening wind brought a new chill with it. Tired, they decided to return to their campsite as soon as the moon rose to provide some light and turned in after a large meal of bread, smoked meat, and cheese, vowing to cook a proper meal the next night.

The next day, the Gracies moved their camp as far westward as they had scouted the day before and pitched camp, leaving a few hours of daylight for them to explore. Huw suggested they leave their horses behind, proceeding on foot along the tree line. Without the sounds of their horses to forewarn others of their approach and their natural stealthy movement, they had a better chance of being unobserved.

'Very well,' said Reggie. 'But we will not be able to cover much ground this way.'

'I believe that it is the nature of our search, not its scope, that may prove more useful, so let us try this today,' said Huw.

Like all Gracies, they moved quietly, even more so when they were trying to be silent. Huw did not play his whistle regularly, but only at even intervals when they were still and immobile, hoping to call the Gemwings to him. Periodically, they would pause and listen for the sound of anything unusual but neither saw nor heard anything aside from some birds and a grazing deer. The Gracies glided through the bracken and underbrush; the small ferns that grew on the forest floor aided their quest for silence as the fronds diffused even the tiny sounds from their feet, shod in supple deer-hide. This, along with the pine needles underfoot, made the Gracies nearly inaudible. Pausing for a late snack, they conversed in low voices and then proceeded westward until the rising of the moon.

They turned back and were headed toward camp, when Rolly brought them up short with a hand gesture. Ahead of them the path's normal shadows flickered and moved with an unfamiliar shape. Quietly creeping toward it, the Gracies saw it was indeed a huge dragonfly. The insect was flitting just above their heads, its outstretched wings easily six feet wide: the Gemwing of myth. Not knowing what to do, the Gracies turned to look at Huw, and he gestured for them to stay motionless. Then Huw slowly withdrew his knife from its sheath at his side and tossed to the ground far beyond his reach. At another gesture from him, the other Gracies did the same. Berwyn was nearly overcome with terror as the great glinting form hovered wraithlike above on the path, its wings fluttering constantly and giving off a faint hum.

Huw raised his face to the Gemwing as he slowly lowered his arms to his side, seeking some sort of clue as to how to communicate with the creature. 'What do I do now?' he asked himself, wishing that the Bubbler had been more forthcoming.

The Gemwing flew closer and closer to Huw, its crystal wings reflecting the moonlight in all different hues, dividing the pale ethereal light into the colors of the rainbow. The Gracies were able to see the insect better now. Its elongated body was graceful and slender, in gray, mottled hues. Huw paused as the dragonfly approached. It grasped his face with its slender legs, its enormous eyes suddenly lighting up from inside, glowing gold and green. A sharp, impossibly thin proboscis emerged from its mouth, penetrating Huw's forehead. For a moment, Huw's composure left him, and he cried out and began to fight the dragonfly, but he then regained himself and stood as still as a stately oak. Several minutes passed by, until the giant dragonfly, whose wings had stopped beating as its legs clutched Huw's head, suddenly withdrew its proboscis. Then, without warning, a small jet of fire emerged from its mouth. This tongue of deep violet flame licked color at Huw's forehead briefly but brightly. With that, the dragonfly was gone, flitting back into the edge of the forest.

Huw would have fallen if his companions had not caught him and held him. For several moments, the other Gracies were shocked and silent, but then in cautious voices they began whispering to Huw, trying to bring him around. As an enormous dark lump formed on his forehead, their voices took on a more determined tone.

'Hush, that damn giant bug might attack us next,' said Berwyn. 'Here, let's start carrying him back to camp. Maybe he will wake up so that he can tell us what to do. Pick up our knives. We will need them.'

Since no one had a better idea, and all were afraid that the Gemwing might return at any moment, they agreed to this plan. As they neared their camp, Huw came groggily awake.

'Sleep, I need to sleep,' he said.

'Then put one foot forward and then the other,' retorted Berwyn, whose arms were aching terribly from supporting his friend. 'It's called walking.' His brisk tone belied fear and anger. Not only had his best friend been attacked by a giant insect, but the welt on Huw's forehead was swelling enormously, and they were far from help and home.

Walking quickly but quietly, they passed along the pathway through the forest like a swift swallow in the night breeze. In less than fifteen minutes, they were at their camp. Huw muttered that he was hungry, and Berwyn, taking charge of their little group, told Rolly to help him prepare a hearty meal while

Reggie, who knew the most about tending wounds and sickness, would look after Huw.

They quickly fed the banked ashes of their fire, and it was then that they first noticed their baggage had been disturbed. Muttering about this in a soft voice, Berwyn noticed that the ground appeared to be wet where their campsite was: too wet for the wind and sun that had been through the small fir trees that sheltered their camp. Holding his hand up to the firelight, Berwyn saw that it was red and sticky with blood. He showed this to Reggie, who looked around the campsite and soon found what he presumed to be a large ball of mud and gravel. This he picked up ... then dropped with a shrill cry, for it was the severed head of a Man.

Staring about them, the Gracies—except for Huw, who was unconscious again—reached for their knives. The fire gave a sudden flicker, and they saw the shadow of a tall seated figure on a rock limned against the moon, its countenance hidden in a dark cloak.

'What have you done here? Who are you?' demanded Berwyn of the figure.

'They were waiting for you to return, to finish robbing you,' the figure said, a male by the deep mellifluous tone of voice, though of what race was not plain. He spoke in an accent that Berwyn could not place. 'They gathered many of your belongings along the river's edge in their boat. Your belongings are still there, but the Men are not. They brought axes and weapons with them. As to who I am, when your friend regains consciousness, ask him.'

Communicating by means of the Gracie hand signals, Rolly said, 'Clearly Men came to raid our camp, meaning to kill us or take us hostage.'

'Yes, but how do we know he's not the cleverest of the lot, just waiting to kill us and rob us?' asked Berwyn with gestures of his own.

'We don't, but as tall and quiet as he is, he could have killed us all and taken our goods and gear. Let's sit down and just ignore him. Maybe he will tell us something,' said Reggie.

Reggie cleared his throat and spoke aloud. 'We owe you thanks for protecting us and our goods. Will you not tell us your name and where you come from?'

'My name would mean nothing to any of you except for Huw. My place of origin is irrelevant. Suffice to say that I am here for the same reason you are: to help the Gemwings.'

'The what?' began Rolly in a poor attempt at subterfuge.

The silent figure said nothing, but began moving his hands inside his cloak.

Fearing they were about to be attacked, Berwyn demanded in no polite tone, 'Who are you? Clearly you know Huw and are not surprised to see him here.'

Drawing his knife, Berwyn and the other Gracies stood protectively over their unconscious friend.

'Please put away your knives,' said the cloaked figure in that same strange rich accent. 'You will not need to hold such arguments with me, and little would your clumsy weapons avail you if you used them.'

'Arrogant, isn't he?' asked a clearly perturbed Berwyn, who counted himself an expert with his knife, particularly when throwing it.

Seeing the figure begin to rise from its seated position, the tension and frustration that had built up all night overcame Berwyn's mind, and, with a flick of his wrist, he sent his knife hurtling at the stranger.

In response, all the Gracies saw was the figure's arm returning to his side. None of them saw how the sword at his side had leapt from its scabbard to deflect Berwyn's knife into the woods. Nor had they seen how the return stroke neatly severed the cord holding Berwyn's traveling cloak around his throat without cutting the skin underneath. All of that happened too fast for their minds to process what their eyes had witnessed. Only when Berwyn's cloak fluttered to the ground did they realize what had just taken place.

'My little friends,' said the imposing figure, 'please sit and tell me your tale. I have medicine and herbs in my pouch that will aid your friend. Bring me some hot water from that kettle.'

Having little choice, Rolly fetched the hot water requested by the mysterious stranger, while Berwyn returned to his protective position over Huw. The welt on Huw's forehead had grown worse. The swelling had increased, and now there were dark red streaks that had not been present before.

As he steeped various herbs in the bowl of hot water brought to him by Rolly, the figure's face was hidden under the hood of his cloak. He produced a short wooden rod from his cloak that glittered at each end. This he began rotating and spinning, generating a soothing sound from the crystals on each end of the rod now revealed in the moonlight. Green light came from the circles that the wand made, and the light coalesced and shined down in slender shafts toward the small bowl containing the steeping herbs. The water bubbled and hissed, though no steam rose from it.

As the Gracies looked on in wonder, the figure changed the focus of the wand, and small jets of green light washed over them. Their weariness and fear began to fade. Berwyn settled himself more comfortably upon the ground, Huw's head and shoulders propped in his lap.

The figure soaked a cloth in the bowl and began bathing Huw's forehead with the liquid. A hissing of steam, purple in the firelight, rose from the welt, which began to shrink before the eyes of the astonished Gracies. When Huw began to moan and thrash, the figure bade Berwyn to hold him still and directed Reggie to take over the bathing of his wound while he retrieved something from his pack.

The figure returned with a small phial, the contents of which he poured down Huw's throat. Several more minutes went by with the Gracies waiting expectantly as the figure sat down on a rock close to the fire. Hoping to get a glimpse of this mysterious stranger, the Gracies were disappointed that only his hands with long, elegant fingers were visible.

'Do you think that I might have something to eat and drink?' asked their unknown guest. 'There is nothing more we can do for now.'

'What about our friend?' demanded Berwyn. 'And what about that horrible monster that attacked us!'

'All that can be done for Huw has been done. And you were not attacked by a horrible monster. The Gemwing simply had to communicate the only way that it knew how.'

'By poking a hole in Huw's head? If you hadn't come along, he would be dead by now!' shouted Berwyn.

'He would not have died, but it would have taken days for the swelling to go down and for Huw to regain his senses, days we do not have.'

Spluttering in anger and frustration, Berwyn did not know what to do, so he remained seated, silently imploring his friend to waken. The welt had nearly disappeared, and the angry red streaks were rapidly fading as well. Huw began murmuring under his breath in a language that none of the Gracies could understand.

Reggie and Rolly, meanwhile, went about preparing a vegetable stew, as they did not know if the figure ate meat like normal people or was odd like Huw. Rolly passed a plate of stew to the figure and to Berwyn, then poured generous amounts of wine into their pewter travel mugs, one of which they offered to the figure. He ate with a bit of a grimace but seemed to enjoy his wine a bit more. Huw repeated the same foreign words and phrases again and again.

Laughing lightly, the figure said, 'He never did get the cadence of that poem right. Even now I can hear him practice and still make the same mistake. Wake up, my little friend, for there is much to be done.'

'I have not got the cadence wrong,' muttered Huw with his eyes still tightly shut. 'That stew smells wonderful. May I have some?' And then he opened his eyes.

'Huw!' cried Berwyn. 'We thought you were going to die!'

'So did I, until I tasted the Elven elixir in my mouth.'

'Elven elixir … What are you talking about?' demanded Berwyn. 'Do you mean that this killer is an Elf?'

'Yes, he is an Elf, but why do you say he is a killer?'

After Berwyn explained, Huw asked the figure, 'I take it that there was nothing else that you could have done?'

'Ever tried to reason with a greedy mercenary bent on murder and theft?' asked the figure rhetorically. 'The pacifistic arguments of you Gracies are wonderfully ineffective outside of Platonia. No, to answer your question, there was no other alternative. Now, my friend, you must eat and regain your strength.'

'Well,' said Berwyn, 'now that you have had your little reunion, could you tell us who this Elf is, where he is from, what happened to you, and what we are supposed to do now?'

Huw laughed weakly. 'He is Emedius, weapons master of the Elves. I would have learned from him but for our pacific stance on all things involving weapons and violence. Still, he and I became friends while I was in Phoenicia, did we not?' Huw slowly sat up.

'We did indeed,' chuckled Emedius darkly, 'but this friendship was strained a bit tonight, as one of your friends had the nerve to attack me.'

Emedius explained his initial encounter with the Gracies, and when he was done, Huw responded, 'Well, did you identify yourself and tell them who you are and where you came from? Of course not, that would have been too easy. Serves you right that Berwyn threw a knife at you! Imagine what it must be like for us peaceful folk to pick up the severed head of a Man in our own camp in our own land and then see a mysterious figure sitting around the remnants of your campfire.'

'That's right,' said Berwyn. 'I still don't trust him. Let him show his face to prove he's an Elf.'

'Emedius, if you would not mind,' said Huw.

Emedius pulled back his hooded cloak and leaned into the firelight. The clear chiseled features of a Greater Elf were there, long blond hair pulled back from his head and held in place with multiple hair rings as befitted a weapons master. Blue eyes revealing strength and truth were set beneath a smooth brow; only fine wrinkles from five thousand years under the sun testified to an age any greater than thirty or so years. There was an ethereal beauty to Emedius' features that could not be falsified, and even Berwyn had to admit that Emedius was an Elf, even though he only had descriptions in books and Huw's tales to go on.

'Why are you here?' demanded Berwyn. 'You still have not explained that, even if you are an Elf.'

'I thought that was clear,' responded Emedius. 'I am here to look after you and see that your mission, now that it has begun, does not fail.'

'Mission! What mission?' demanded Berwyn. 'We came to the plateau to help these giant bugs, and all we have received for our troubles is an attack on Huw, a campsite full of blood, and an arrogant Elf telling us we have a mission.'

'Our mission,' said Emedius, 'is to transport the Gemwings safely to the Emerald Vale.'

'Why—'

'If you will let me finish,' said Emedius with just a hint of impatience, 'I will then answer any of your questions. As I was saying, we are here to save the Gemwings. I know that you have met them by the unique mark upon Huw's forehead: a mark last seen a millennia ago by those willing to help them during a great time of need. We will need to transport them. I have brought special enclosures for them that will keep out the light of the sun, while still allowing them fresh air. All I know is that the Gemwings are vital somehow to the Magi of the Vale, who summoned me and sent me here to aid you, and by removing them from here to there, we can save not only the Gemwings but apparently have a profound effect on the future of Nostraterra.'

'But what are these Gemwings?' persisted Berwyn. 'Where do they come from, and why are they here? I can't begin to understand how these great insects have such an important place in the affairs of the world. Why should we help you or them?'

'The Gemwings are an ancient sentient race of insects travelling throughout Nostraterra,' said Emedius. 'There are flowers that grow here on the plateau that grow nowhere else in the known world, and these flowers are necessary for the Gemwings to mate. Every hundred years, during high summer, they travel here to mate before returning to the Vale. After mating they visit your Well of Life, recharging its magic somehow and feasting on the pale yellow lilies that are their only source of food outside the Emerald Vale. That they are still here months after they were supposed to leave is quite confusing. You Gracies did not remove their flowers, did you?'

'No,' said Huw. 'They were destroyed early last summer by a man, and we have only a few bulbs stored near the gardens that were replanted this spring. They have not yet bloomed. We also have no idea how a man could cross the river into Platonia.'

'I suspect that man came the same way that these men did. There is a narrow section of the river just north of here, and earlier tonight, I watched the men I eventually slew throw a rope and grapnel from the high cliff-side and catch it in the tops of a tree on this side of the Beadle. They sent the smallest member of their group across first and he brought other ropes with him, enabling the rest of the gang to join them. But returning to the flowers, if a Man destroyed the flowers here in Platonia, then perhaps the other flowers growing between here and the Vale were also destroyed. The Gemwings must have become trapped here.'

Berwyn began to mutter again, when Emedius said, 'Right, let's try this again with more clarity, my impatient assailant. The Gemwings are responsible for maintaining the magic in your Well of Life. No Gemwings, no magic well. With no magic well, your Bubblers would be gone within a year or so, and then who would help you keep out the brigands and squatters that covet your lands? Would you place your trust wholly in Men? I think not! Your kind knows better than all others what happens when a superior force wants what you have.'

To this, Berwyn had nothing to say and confined his protests to mutterings under his breath.

'Come, let us enjoy the fire and your food and wine,' said Emedius. 'Tomorrow will be a busy day.'

'Are you alone?' asked Huw.'

'I came alone to your camp,' said Emedius. I have a few other friends waiting at East Point and South Point for our arrival.'

Nodding his head, Huw was suddenly overcome with a terrible headache. His eyes rolled back into his head, and he began to twitch and moan unintelligibly.

'Do something!' demanded Berwyn of Emedius.

'There is nothing that I can do that I have not done already.'

'What is happening to him?'

'I do not know!' responded Emedius angrily rising from his rock to crouch at Huw's side. 'Help me hold him. Hopefully the fit will pass soon.'

As the Gracies moved to comply, Huw's fit ended as quickly as it began. Coming to himself, Huw begged Reggie for a mug of wine. Draining the mug in two gulps, Huw set the mug down.

'What happened, Huw?' asked Berwyn.

'The Gemwing made contact with my mind, assuring itself that I am truly the person it believes that I am, and that I can save it and its kind from extinction.'

'Extinction!' exclaimed Rolly. 'What are you saying?'

'I am saying that the Gemwing and its mate are the last of its kind. The rest have perished here on the plateau or in the vast lands between here and the Vale. Their entire race, nearly a thousand of them, flew here to mate, only to find after mating that their only food source outside the Emerald Vale, in our gardens, was destroyed. They slowly starved to death here on this plateau, but before each Gemwing died, it transferred the last of its life energies to the older, more powerful Gemwings in turn, until only these last two are left. This transfer of power allowed the remaining pair to mate and create one last cache of eggs in hopes that even if all the Gemwings perished, someone could take the eggs back to the Vale. Without adults to teach future offspring, it is unlikely that the Gemwings that might hatch from their eggs will know how to preserve our Well, much less carry on their other magical functions. Thankfully, one last male and female Gemwing exist. We will take them the day after tomorrow, along with the future of their race, to the Emerald Vale.'

'Race, what race?' asked an angry, thoroughly flustered Berwyn. 'They are insects, no more. Granted they are one hundred times the size of their nearest kin, but they are no more important than moths who circle around a candle or lantern in the dark.'

'Rarely have you uttered a more boorish statement,' replied Huw heatedly. 'These 'insects' as you call them are sentient, possessed of independent thought, and are the key to the survival of life that you cannot comprehend, bearers of magic that is beyond any in Nostraterra. If you cannot offer anything constructive, please remain silent. Clean the dishes then go to bed; I have no more words for you tonight.'

Speechless, Berwyn had no idea how and why he had irritated his friend so greatly. Meekly, he turned to the dishes and glasses. Trudging back and forth to the river, he and Reggie and Rolly cleaned up, pouring more wine for Emedius, who observed the goings on with a slight smile on his face, while Huw sat glowering in silence.

'Peace, Huw, they do not have the knowledge of your contact with the Gemwings,' said Emedius at last. 'They do not know what you know, so forgive them their ignorance. They will know soon enough what is at risk and why our mission is so desperate.'

'What?' asked Huw, then shook his head and went on. 'Sorry, old friend. It is difficult to keep the thoughts of the Gemwings out of my mind.' He turned to Berwyn. 'I am sorry, Berwyn. I spoke too harshly. I have knowledge that you do not. I will try to explain over the next few days so that you understand. For now, however, you will have to trust me and Emedius when we say that taking the Gemwings to the Vale is paramount to the survival of Platonia.'

Berwyn nodded, at a loss for words.

'Rest, my friend, you will need your strength tomorrow,' said Emedius. He handed Huw a dark phial. 'Drink this and you will have clearer thoughts soon, though you will still hear the thoughts of our friends the Gemwings.'

* * *

The following day, as his friends tended the fire and cooked food, Huw stayed in bed, tossing and turning in his blankets, a greasy sweat upon his bow as his mind fought for supremacy against the thoughts implanted within his brain by the Gemwing. Rolly expressed his concerns, while the other Gracies stood nearby.

'He will live,' Emedius assured them. 'His spirit is strong, and he will be able to accept the thoughts of our winged friends without losing himself in the process. The Gemwings would only trust their safety and their legacy to one who was wholly innocent of taking life. Is it not true that of all among you, only Huw has never consumed meat or fish?'

'That is true,' said Reggie. 'He always said that meat did not agree with him. We had to pack extra potatoes, onions, and grains for him. He is always so thin—we wish that meat did agree with him.'

'Meat does not agree with him, because it signifies death, the suffering of animals or fish so that others can survive. Huw is unique in that he comes from a peaceful people, and within that people he has never taken a life or profited from death. Only someone who is that pure in both thought and deed could have made contact with the Gemwings and engendered their trust. Come let us prepare the cages for our friends. Sunlight will kill them, and they will only come to us at night.'

That night, Huw was able to rise from his bedroll, and Emedius left them for a few moments, moving toward the river. When he returned, he was carrying a stack of boxes that in the firelight were revealed to be cages covered in thick dark cloth. 'Huw will come with me onto the plateau tonight, while you other Gracies pack up your gear so we can leave first thing in the morning.'

Several hours later, when Huw and Emedius returned, the Gracies were amazed by the sight of the Gemwings hovering over Huw's shoulder. Only after Huw placed a large lumpy object that glistened darkly with a brown hue into a separate, smaller box well insulated from light would the Gemwings submit and climb into the cages prepared for them.

The dark covered boxes were ready for departure. A stranger would have noted nothing, but for an unearthly low hum coming from the cages. After checking to make certain the cages were secure, the Gracies turned in for the night.

The next day, they rose at dawn. With Reggie and Rolly carrying one cage, and Huw and Berwyn carrying another, while Emedius took the smaller box, the group proceeded to the river, where they found Rolly's ferry boats waiting for them. Gawking at the impossibly tall and beautiful Elf lord in their midst, the Gracies held their tongues and cast off from the shore. The horses traveled on a separate boat, with the cages placed deep within the cabin in the middle of the boat, safe from prying eyes and questions.

The next morning dawned clear and cool. Thick patches of fog appeared sporadically above the surface of the river. The current was swift and strong, and aided by a strong north wind, the Gracies soon reached the broader part of the river that was the ferry point between the eastern edge of Platonia and the outside world.

Instead of the usual ferry boats plying back and forth, there was a great noise and smoke. Booms echoed from the mists rising from the water, and distant shouts were heard. 'Clear the way!' cried Emedius, pushing the Gracie boat captain from his path as he leapt to the top of the small cabin for a moment to stare ahead.

'Captain, put us ashore immediately; crash the boat onto the bank if you have to,' Emedius demanded. Nearly a half mile above the fords, the boats lurched onto the western shore of the Beadle; the Gemwing boxes were retrieved from below, along with their belongings. Their horses were shoved none too gently into the shallow water and dragged up the side of the bank. Quickly mounting their horses, with the cages securely tied to Huw's mount, the Gracies found a game trail and moved south and west to meet the great road where it ended at the complex of docks and piers from which they had originally departed on this journey. Emedius shouted for them to follow as quickly as they could and ran before them faster than their short horses could manage in such rough terrain.

Reaching the fords, they saw a sight that astounded them. The river was boiling with the forms of the Bubblers and with swift boats filled with brigands who were trying to force their way across the Beadle. As soon as a boat was swamped or turned over, a glowing hissing ball would be flung from the brigands on the far shore. The ball would drift upon the waters for a few moments before it would explode with devastating force, spreading a greenish liquid that seemed to destroy the river spirits.

Blasting fire was known to the Gracies as a compound created by the alchemists of Men, but this green liquid that spread along the surface of the river was something wholly new. Where the liquid touched overhanging willow branches the trees immediately sickened and turned black. Fish by the hundreds floated to the surface, and other river creatures, including muskrats, otters, and even insects, suffered the same fate, covering the surface of the river in a terrible panoply of death. Nothing could come into contact with this terrible green liquid and survive, and the Gracies could see it steadily spread from the exploding balls tossed into the river. Clearly the Bubblers were losing this fight, the waters becoming calmer under the sickly green sheen as the brigands' boats, staying upstream of the poison, pulled closer to the shores of Platonia.

Emedius cried aloud in the Elven tongue for his fellow Elves to come to him. Twelve Elves arrived almost immediately, appearing as if out of nowhere. Emedius ordered five of them to defend the Bubblers with arrows, while he told another, Nirdan, an Elven wizard, to use his magic to attack the brigands.

'My Lord,' stammered Nirdan, 'I brought crystals for weather and healing, not for war. I do not know how I can be of help.'

'Do you not, Nirdan?' asked a clearly vexed Emedius. 'Many battles have been decided by weather. Prepare your magic accordingly and thwart the enemy as best you can. Trust that the air spirits whose magic is summoned and focused through all of our crystals will come to our aid. Here is the wand of healing that I brought with me. If I do not return, you must make certain these Gracies escape and that the boxes on these horses reach the Emerald Vale. The rest of you lay down arrow fire into the boats, but target particularly the alchemist of Men if you can find him. I will prepare the Gracies for our trip south.'

'But the Gracies refuse to let us use violence within their land and demand that we speak to the brigands instead,' replied the Elven Wizard.

'Did the Gracies try diplomacy first?' asked Emedius.

'Yes, Lord. Their messenger was killed, his headless body sent back tied to his horse. It was then that the battle began this morning,' replied the wizard.

'While I sympathize with our peaceful friends, Platonia cannot be lost. Nor can our mission fail. Do as I asked. I will address the Gracies' concerns in a moment,' said Emedius.

Fanning out along the river's edge, the Elves launched their arrows across the water, slaying the entire crew of three boats about to land in Platonia.

Meanwhile Nirdan removed a long staff from his pack, with a bright crystal on both ends of the staff. Hoisting it above his head, moving it in a complicated rhythm, he first began reciting the spell in his mind, compelling the air from which he drew his magic to come to his aid. A high-pitched tone of whistling wind arose, and the sound of rain upon the water was heard. Soon the deeper sounds of thunder and lightning commenced, emanating from the wizard as a blue-gray light began to envelop him from the very air. Clouds rushed overhead and began to build and rise, rapidly darkening the skies above the Elven wizard as his chants became audible. Soon the first drops of rain were felt from the towering thundercloud overhead, and a strong brisk wind began to blow out from the base of the storm hovering just over Platonia toward the boats, pushing them back across the river to the far shore.

Now bolts of lightning spattered down from the heavens to strike the near shoreline, running across the ground in actinic blue-white light too swift to be seen. Great cries went up from the brigand camp, and the balls hurled by the alchemist stopped.

The storm began drifting away, but then Nirdan brought the last of his power to bear, calling the clouds back to their place, as their task was unfinished. The lightning struck down more fiercely and desperately than before slaying more of the Men and driving their boats from the river.

This continued for some time, but then Nirdan collapsed in exhaustion, no longer able to hold his spell, his energy spent. No longer under Elven control, the storm began to fade, drifting off to the east in a torrent of rain, with one last cold squall pushing four boats filled with ten men each back against the shore.

Heartened by the storm, the Bubblers returned to sinking the boats, but then the great balls of floating fire came back from across the river. Seeing that he had no choice and that there was no one else to aid the river spirits, Emedius gave final orders to his Elven companions and the Gracies to get out of Platonia at any cost, saving the Gemwings and taking them safely to the Emerald Vale. Leaping into the river, Emedius bounced off of the heads of the Bubblers and the broken shells of the boats disappearing into the mass of brigands on the eastern shore. His two swords flicking and flashing, he slew brigands who climbed over one another trying to escape this beautiful terrible embodiment of death who had suddenly landed in their midst. Weapons reached out to touch him, but they were all turned aside as Emedius bore down upon the alchemist. His fellow Elves supported him, sending nearly a hundred arrows into the midst of the Brigands, slaying at least fifty, casting their ranks into confusion and disarray.

Suddenly a great explosion went up from the brigand camp, and the brigands scattered momentarily, allowing Emedius to retrace his steps, blood seeping from a gash on his left arm.

'Come to me, Gracies,' he cried to those nearby. 'I slew the alchemist, and his weapons are no more, but the river spirits are nearly depleted. You Gracies must hold this shore against the brigands until help can come from outside your lands. I will leave six Elves here to organize your people into defensive lines so that you can keep Platonia safe.'

'But we must not use violence...,' began one of the Gracie elders.

'Yes, you must, or they will ravage your lands and homes, slaying you where they stand. It is time to make a choice between noble principles and practicality. If you do not fight, the six Elves that I leave here with you will fight and eventually die, losing their lives for nothing. You must hold out for a week before aid can come to you. That is the minimum time for a message to reach either the Kozaki or the men of Eldora at their city of Amadeus. We must go now. Take action and soothe your consciences later. Farewell.'

'Do you think that they will fight?' asked a stunned Berwyn.

'I believe so. Look, you can see younger Gracies with hunting bows taking position behind trees. Your people are tougher than many deem. They should hold out until help arrives, but not a moment is to be lost. Quickly, let us depart for the southern merger of the rivers!' But even as he spoke, he swayed on his feet.

Huw remarked, 'You are hurt. You must rest.'

'No, there can be no rest for me,' said Emedius. 'My Elven companion can use the wand of healing on my wound. But even if I die, you must reach the Vale as soon as possible.'

Emedius, despite his weakened state, gathered Huw and his friends. Together they proceeded south and then southwest around Platonia, following game trails laid along the river. They rested for half an hour later that afternoon, and Nirdan used the healing wand carried by Emedius to tend Emedius' wound; the cuts given by an exploding fireball had swollen dramatically, with a foul stench and a dreadful greenish ichor oozing from it. Emedius soon roused them, insisting they take advantage of the few hours remaining before sunset.

The next day, Emedius forced the Gracies to their feet, demanding they move as quickly as possible. Muscles aching, they led their horses through the thick brush and then rode them along ancient grasslands.

Nearly delirious from his wounds, which, had proved more resilient than expected, thwarting the efforts of Nirdan, Emedius led them to the Elven encampment shortly before sunset near to where the Beadle came together again, forming the southernmost point of Platonia. Six other Elves were waiting there. They grabbed Emedius as he collapsed, preventing him from striking the ground. Nirdan used the healing wand again, and Emedius' health improved enough to permit him to drink from the phials given to him by Nirdan. He soon fell into a fitful sleep.

Nirdan said, 'I have never seen the like of such a poison. He must return to Phoenicia for proper treatment, and even then I am not sure that the Elven healers can save him. We must move as swiftly as possible.'

The twelve Elves that accompanied them were busy breaking camp, moving the packs from the exhausted horses of the Gracies onto their own steeds. Much greater in stature and speed, the Elven horses stood gazing intelligently at the Gracies, awaiting their turn to have the small, unfamiliar saddles and packs placed upon them. Loading the Gracies and horses onto the boats drawn up on the shore, Nirdan moved this small convoy off the shore into the swift current, as the Gracies' horses looked forlorn at losing their masters' company.

Journeying down the swift river, Nirdan led the Gracies into the heart of the Dark Forest, demanding that all of the Elves and the Gracies row down the river as fast as possible. An ancient survivor of woods that was as old as Platonia, the forest had a magic of its own. Its boundaries were inviolate, and anyone who breached its borders never emerged again. Here were some of the tallest trees in Nostraterra, surpassed only by the legendary trees of the Emerald Vale.

The Gracies were uneasy passing down the swift river with these trees towering hundreds of feet above them, a canyon of dark trunks and green canopies. The occasional bird could be seen flitting from tree to tree, and the small sounds of squirrels sounding their typical alarm cries could be heard, but otherwise there was silence.

Nirdan bade the Gracies to begin fishing over the sides of the boats in order to catch their dinner while he tended to Emedius. More phials and more use of the crystal wand seemed to allow Emedius to hold his own against the poison. The Gemwings remained in their cages, sipping the nectar gathered for them sparingly and sipping the water that was placed into their cages at night. Occasionally the Gemwings asked questions of Huw through his mind, but all he could tell them as he busied himself within the boat was that they were on the way to the Vale.

Clearing the forest later that day, the Elves took the boats ashore on the eastern bank. Reggie and Rolly both felt smug, as they had caught many large fish, pike and perch for the most part, with one old brown trout thrown into the mix.

Cooking their fish upon the fire, with spices from their mess kits, the Gracies shared their fish with the Elves, who opened their own packs to distribute wine, bread, and dried fruits. Nirdan mixed a strong potion and, with the help of Berwyn, had Emedius drink it. With a great shudder and a moan, the weapons master fell swiftly asleep. Huw ate a simple vegetable stew he prepared for himself.

'Rest now, my little friends,' said Nirdan. 'There is time enough for questions, but know that on the morrow we ride as fast as our steeds will carry us for the Emerald Vale. The Gemwings cannot last much longer.'

'What of Emedius?' asked Huw, gesturing at the Elf, who had fallen into a fitful sleep. Streaks of red and green ran across his face.

'We shall divide our group,' said Nirdan. 'Six Elves, including myself, will continue toward Phoenicia with Emedius. The remaining six Elves will conduct you to the Vale. The Gemwings are much more important than the life of a single Elf, even Emedius.'

Chapter Two

Renaissance

When Huw woke the next morning, he saw that Emedius was slightly more coherent and asked him about the Gemwings and why they were taking them to the Vale.

'You did not read all the books in our vast library,' answered the weapons master. 'If you had, you would have learned a bit more about the Gemwings, but not everything.'

'What don't I know?' persisted Huw.

'The only relevant information I have is that the Gemwings are vital sources of magical renewal, such as renewing your well. How they relate specifically to the Vale, the Magi will not say. The Magi only told me that without the Gemwings, much of the good magic still left in Nostraterra will pass away. That was all we needed to know. With the ascension of Men as the preeminent power in Nostraterra, with their history of greed, war, and destruction, it will take all of the good magic left to all the races to restore a balance.'

With this last revelation, Emedius slumped back onto this bedroll, and three Elves with extra horses slung Emedius onto a spare horse.

Nirdan said, 'You must fly for the entrance of the Vale. If the riders of Kozak find you, they will not oppose you, but you must not tarry with them. The Gemwings have little time left.' Seeing the questions in Huw's face, he added, 'I don't know if he will survive, but I will send word to Platonia as soon as his fate is clear. May the Air Spirits guide you and guard you from harm.'

'May the Air Spirits show you the way when no path seems right,' replied Huw formally, concluding the parting ceremony of the Greater Elves.

Their new escort leader, Carlin, spoke in the common speech. 'We tarry not.'

As they mounted the Elvish horses, Berwyn turned to Huw and asked, 'How much did you know, Huw, prior to our leaving for the plateau?'

'Nothing that I did not tell you,' Huw answered in exasperation. 'Yes, I learned much in Phoenicia, but little did I learn of the Gemwings, but for the fact that they possessed an unknown magic and that it aided Platonia in some fashion. As we all suspected, I thought they might be dangerous, perhaps deadly, but with our well failing, what choice did we have? Should we place our survival over the safety of Platonia? If I was wrong, then yes, we would have died, but I was not, so please stop complaining. Besides, who can say? By saving the Gemwings, we might be rewarded by the Magi of the Vale.'

'Reward, what reward?' asked Berwyn. 'Here we are, miles from our home, bound to some mysterious place called the Emerald Vale to take two enormous insects as passengers, while our land is attacked by brigands. If that were not bad enough, my brother is running the inn, Rolly's business is running itself, and Reggie's father needs help from outside Platonia or all our homes might be burnt.'

'We are riding toward that help as we speak,' said Huw. 'The riders of Kozak patrol this country; it is likely that we will meet them in our dash across the plains of Kozak before we get to the Emerald Vale. We must ride before the Gemwings perish and Platonia with them. The Magi may be able to help us, perhaps sending one of their Order to help guard our lands. I heard rumors in Phoenicia of creatures allied with the Magi, called the Vespre that can change form and are deadly when provoked. If we are truly fortunate, the Magi might send us magical aid. If not, then we must hope that the Gemwings survive and can restore our Well of Life before the year is out.'

'The Magi may be able to help you indeed,' interjected Carlin in the Elvish speech, addressing Huw. 'The balance in Nostraterra has shifted quite abruptly in the past few years, and not to the good. The Magi could slow the felling of the forests and the hunting of the beasts. The recent messages from Marcellus show that Men are increasing at a great rate, and forests, especially the last remnants of the ancient forests, are being cleared for lumber and crop lands. Certain animals, particularly the fur bearers, are being hunted out of existence.

'There is little we Great Elves can do, as our numbers are so small. Only our distant cousins in the forests could actually be a force that Men have to reckon with. There, Men have been checked and forced to leave the Great Forest and the Northern Forest and its surrounding confines alone. This has only diverted

Men into easier lands to conquer and transform into farms and pastures, and this, combined with the current political situation in Eldora, is worrisome indeed. Now let us ride swiftly, as your very survival depends upon our success.'

They began their dash across the plains of Kozak, heading southeast toward the entrance to the Emerald Vale. They hoped that they would be able to cross the plains in three days, bringing the Gemwings to safety within the Vale. Early during their first day, they met with outriders and scouts from Kozak, and while they were allowed to proceed, the baggage horses slowed them, and at sunset they were met by a captain of Kozak who politely asked their business and their names. Astounded by wonder, for no Gracies had left Platonia for over a thousand years, but for the expedition to destroy Magnar, the Kozaki captain was equally amazed to find Greater Elves in the saddles before him. He invited them to visit the King.

Politely, but desperately, Huw replied, 'We have an errand first with the Magi of the Emerald Vale, but we could come to the King of Kozak after.'

'Nonsense,' replied the captain. 'The King is recently returned to his court, and he could not abide our story if we told him the Gracies of old had ridden forth to his land and had not enjoyed his hospitality.'

'But our errand is most urgent, and it will be lost if we do not come to the Emerald Vale in three days!' exclaimed Huw. 'Our lives and those of our loved ones are at stake!'

'Fortunately, I can perform my duty and honor yours at the same time. We will take you on our horses, the fastest in Nostraterra, even including these magnificent horses of the Elves. We will be able to exchange these mounts with rested horses as well, so you will be able to gallop all the way to Mostyn, which is close to the Emerald Vale at this time of year. With the good will of the King, you will be able to arrive at the Vale ahead of your schedule, and all throughout the land will be honored by your visit.'

Sensing this battle over protocol was lost and could not be won, Huw acquiesced, and the Gracies rode at a tremendous pace toward Mostyn and the Vale. Arriving at Mostyn, they answered the polite questions of their hosts, and messengers presaged their arrival at the court of the Kozaki king.

Immediately upon arrival, they were taken before King Bernadus, who greeted them with full ceremony, stating, 'Here are the descendants of the Gracies of old, who gave their lives along with Men, Dwarves, and Elves to defeat the terrible shadow. Let us praise them!'

Joining Bernardus at his high table in the great hall, the Gracies were treated as honored guests, food and drink set before them as they climbed onto tall chairs prepared with high cushions to accommodate their short stature. Oil lamps and candles provided yellow light, and for the first time since leaving Platonia, the Gracies began to relax.

After giving many toasts, Bernadus asked the Gracies, 'Why have you paid us the honor of journeying to our land after so many years of silence between our peoples?'

'Alas, Lord, we have tidings both glad and sad. Those that are glad shall be first told to the recipients, the Magi of the Emerald Vale,' replied Huw.

Puzzled but still in good humor from his mead, Bernadus asked, 'What of the sad news?'

'Well, Lord, our land of Platonia was attacked three days ago by hundreds of Men. An alchemist of the Westmen was also present, destroying the Bubblers, the river spirits who protect us, with a blasting fire and poison. We left in the midst of the battle, and you know my people are not warriors and indeed despise war. But war has come to us, it seems, and we are in dire need of aid.'

'What'¿exclaimed an astonished Bernadus. 'Do you tell me that the land of the Gracies, of the very folk that aided our great grandsire in his war against the Great Darkness; is in danger because of Men?'

'Yes, Lord.' said Huw. At Bernadus' bidding, he described the battle more fully.

Muttering under his breath, Bernadus thought for a few minutes. Then: 'Assemble my War Council,' he roared. 'This shall not go unpunished.'

'Peace, my Lord,' said one of his counselors, a man named Flardon. 'This is a matter for Eldora, not for us. It is their law that has been broken, not ours.'

'So, you are a common lawyer,' said the king with contempt. 'Would you split hairs on the edge of a sword as barbarians were coming for your wife and children?'

'Nay, Lord,' sputtered Flardon. 'That is not what I meant.'

'What did you mean then?' demanded Bernadus.

'The treaty of protection of Platonia was signed by Eldora, not us. It is their responsibility to honor their agreements. Any action on our part could be interpreted as usurping Eldoran power,' replied Flardon. Some around the table murmured their assent, while others shook their heads.

'Is it not true that Platonia was given to the Gracies by the King of Eldora in perpetuity for their services in the Great War?'

'Yes, Lord, it was,' replied Flardon.

'And now the Gracies say their ancient borders are penetrated, attacked, and coveted by the filth of squatters, those half-castes and layabouts we have thrown from our very borders?' asked the King.

'Yes, Lord,' replied Flardon.

'Therefore, if we help enforce the decrees of the Kings of Eldora, how are we in the wrong?' asked Bernadus.

'When you phrase it like that, Lord, I believe that the laws of the ancient Kings of Eldora are still in effect,' said Flardon with a skeptical look on his face.

'Well, we are in agreement, then,' cried a happy Bernadus. 'If we send riders to the aid of the Gracies, then we are simply aiding the Men of Eldora with their duties and honoring an ancient treaty.'

Realizing that Bernadus' logic was without flaw, but fraught with political implications, Flardon stated, 'Yes, it is true on paper, but the real implications are somewhat different.'

'I care not for those who would transform the realm of Kozak into a decadent society bereft of honor and filled with vice. Let ten *Faris* go forth tonight under the banners of both the Kings of Eldora and of Kozak; have them clear the borders of Platonia for at least five leagues on the eastern side. Meanwhile, we shall send a messenger to our brother king, Creon of Eldora, informing him of all that has happened here. If there are ill feelings from Creon, I will deal with them. But the main thing is to see that our friends here have the support they require before it is too late.'

The Gracies profusely thanked Bernardus, who gracefully acknowledged their gratitude and said, 'While there are some who have forgotten the debt owed to you Gracies, I have not. Any aid I can give you today is but small recompense for your deeds of valor and honor.'

* * *

The next morning, the Gracies were carried with the same extreme rapidity toward the Emerald Vale. This time they were conducted by riders both before and behind to clear their way across the lush plains of Kozak. Reaching the end of daylight, the escort pitched camp, with only Berwyn complaining about a lack of proper bedding and a proper inn. Laughing, their honor guard captain said, 'You little folk have gotten too comfortable with your lives. Live on the open plains for a winter with only your pack and your horse to keep you company; you will know discomfort. You will also soon see that you need little else to survive.'

'Survival is all well and good, but how does being hungry, cold and tired help you?' retorted Berwyn.

'It reminds you of who you are,' replied the captain. 'It strips away the veneer of society, forcing you to confront not only the elements but the elemental parts of yourself, to get to really know yourself.'

Puzzled, Berwyn looked around and was rescued by Huw, who said, 'I take it you were once a scholar, perhaps of the royal family, and that you tired of books?'

Chuckling deeply, he said, 'Guilty as charged. I am Rupert, second cousin to the King, and I went to Eldora and studied the ancient lore and histories so I could bring it back to Kozak to teach others. Shortly I realized that while knowledge was well and good, we were in danger of forgetting our heritage, forgetting our history. After completing my studies, I returned to Mostyn and spent a year teaching our wise men the secrets lost in the past. Then I renounced land and title and announced my desire to venture forth to the Northern Vale beyond the Shale Mountains, to meet our distant kin. My family thought I was mad; all that was my birthright was thrown away in their eyes, and some questioned my ability to reason any more. The King's father, however, went riding with me one day, and we talked of my thoughts. I told him of my desire to return to where we had come from and that I did not believe that Eldora and its culture were right for those of us that lived on the plains.

'He didn't agree or disagree, but instead named me ambassador to the tribes of the North Vale and sent me forth with a Faris of our most traditional riders. Long weeks did we have on our journey, for the pathways north had become vague and overgrown. We found our distant cousins, and it gave me great pleasure to hear our tongue spoken correctly for the first time with the northern accent that has virtually disappeared from the land. Many hard contests did we have, and much did we have to prove with horse, bow, and sword before they would speak to us as equals.' Here Rupert rubbed his left shoulder with the memory of an ancient injury.

'Well, we returned to Mostyn, and we told of our northern cousins to the King. He asked if I wanted to return as the permanent ambassador. I told him no,

I missed the open plain, the hissing of the wind through the grasses. I wanted to simply be a captain of Kozak, no longer second Komandir of the Army, unless war befell us. The King's father looked me in the eye and granted my request. That was nearly fifty years ago, and soon I shall go to my long rest with my forefathers. But I have spent my days on the open fields between the mountains and the rivers, living the life a rider should lead.'

Not knowing what to say, the Gracies were quiet for a while, until Huw asked, 'What about your northern cousins made them different from you?'

'There was a purity; a lack of pretense,' said Rupert. 'They knew who and what they were. They tended their horses and grew their crops in their short season, trading with other Men, Dwarves, and even Elves for their needs the land could not supply. Every day they rose and assembled into Faris and rode their narrow land between the Mountains and the river, vigilant for the least discrepancy in their surroundings. They have grown over the past two centuries and have expanded throughout the entire vale, and there in the bitter cold of the northern winters they still send their young men out on survival marches to prove their mettle.

'Some of the women go along, too, Valkyrja who are as deadly with lance and sword as any man. Those who survive become the riders of the next generation, fending off the fell creatures of the Mountains, keeping the wolves and the great cats from the horse studs. Each month there were contests of horsemanship, marksmanship, skill with the lance and sword. Each night, the sagas of their history would be told and sung around the fires, the memories of those who had gone before kept alive by those of the present.

'When I returned to Kozak, all I could see were the dandies of the land who had gone to Titania and had been softened by the ways of Eldora, wenching and gambling into the night. They had little honor, and many of them could no longer ride easily. If pressed to ride for a day, they could barely move the next. Every time I am back at court, I see that the old values have slipped a little further and that we are one step closer to forgetting our roots in the north.'

'Wasn't your mission successful? You seem very popular with our escort,' said Huw.

Smiling, the captain said, 'Yes, I was somewhat successful, and many of our riders now actually are riders in the truest sense of the word, able to blend themselves with their horse as our forefathers did against the shadow, and in this I have the King's support, for he is similar to his father. Always there are men of comfort, however, men of ease who want fine meats and wine and a comfortable bed every night, who fight me for the King's authority. Today there are men of money who claim they own certain parts of the plains, forbidding others entry unless they pay a fee to graze their horses. I and those like me have little use for them, and, but for the King's desire for peace and prosperity, I and those like me would cleanse the kingdom of them in a day. Perhaps your arrival as legends out of the songs will aid those of us determined to preserve Kozak for what it was and should be. It is late, however, and we must be up with the sun if you want to arrive at the Emerald Vale tomorrow,' said Rupert.

'Thank you for your tale,' replied Huw. 'Much of what you have said now makes sense to me. I will have one last sip of wine and turn in.'

Nothing remarkable happened that night. The only sounds, aside from the soft noises of the horses and the snores of the men of Kozak, were the sounds of the wind through the grasses. The next morning, all were ready early, as Carlin and Huw tended to the Gemwings in their covered cages. Breakfasting early and riding northwest along the plain, they soon came to the river Wyryn and proceeded to the fords, crossing the river to the west side and taking the ancient road eastward.

Suddenly, while they were in midstream, a force of cavalry burst forth from the trees along both sides of the river and shrill horns sounded. Caught off guard, Rupert made a quick decision, ordering his men not yet in the river to form a rearguard while the men in midstream were to proceed and reinforce the men on the far bank. The brigand cavalry arrayed against them were nearly two hundred, far greater than the one hundred men in a typical Faris of Kozak. The brigands charged from both sides, their tactics clear: to force the Kozaki into the river and trap them there, where their superior skills could not be brought to bear.

'Hold the rear line!' shouted Rupert as twenty-five riders formed into a short semicircle, lances lowered. 'When they come within one hundred paces, charge!'

Now, as the enemy cavalry came closer, Huw could see the tan of the deep desert on the faces of the charging men, but instead of the banners of Shardan, the soldiers flew an unknown banner: blue lightning on a dark background.

Emerging from the water, Rupert formed his leading cavalry into a tight wedge. He bid the wings of his command charge forward and outward, leaving a small gap in the center.

Turning to the Gracies, he said, 'You will ride with my personal guard of ten men. Once we have broken a small hole in their lines, you must make one last dash for the Vale.'

'What of you and your men?' asked Huw.

'My King told me that you must succeed on your mission. If that costs us our lives, then that is our fate. Now be ready!'

The wedge of the riders tightened up their ranks, their spears held high. The opposing formation came charging in one long line, clearly wishing to envelop the Kozaki and force them back into the river, where they would slaughtered. Then, at Rupert's command, the Kozaki cavalry charged into the superior force, dividing into two diagonal lines with a small gap only twenty feet wide at the center, thus forcing the brigands to divide their forces in response.

'Now!' shouted Rupert. At that, the trailing edges of the wedge rode forward, forming smaller wedges on the left and right of the center of their original line. 'Hold,' he said to his personal guard. 'Let our riders attack first.'

The Kozaki wedges lowered their lances and galloped toward their foes, their long spears shattering the initial charge of the brigand horseman. Several Kozaki riders fell from arrows fired from Shardan saddle bows, but Carlin and his fellow Elves answered with blinding speed. Nearly twenty Elven arrows filled the air at the center of the Shardan line, and fifteen of the enemy fell from their saddles, with four others wounded. Briefly, the Shardan line was broken, and a gap nearly fifty yards formed in its center.

'Ride!' cried Rupert. With ten reserve Kozaki riders in addition to his personal guard, the captain charged through the gap. Then, seeing that the Gracies were through the melee and riding hard, Rupert pulled up and turned back toward his men as the wedges began to falter, determined to delay if not prevent any pursuit of the Gracies. 'Go, little folk,' he called. 'Do not forget our valor today!'

The ten riders escorting the Gracies continued to gallop as Rupert and his ten horsemen formed another wedge heading back to the battle, their silver horns blaring into the morning light. The Elves paused for a moment and, seeing that Rupert had turned his wedge toward the left of the original battle line, fired arrow after arrow in a small cloud at the greatest cluster of Shardan horsemen gathered as a great knot amongst the Kozaki riders. Screams and cries came from the Shardan ranks, and Huw had a moment of hope, amazed at this tremendous sacrifice. But knowing that they must not fail, he turned his head from the battle and urged his horse forward again. Half an hour later, they paused to rest their horses and take a bite in the saddle. Soon, however, they heard a distant horn, and it was not Kozaki.

'Fly little ones!' cried the sergeant of their escort. 'Take three of my riders. We will hold them off as long as we can.'

With that, the exhausted and terrified Gracies rode again, leaving their other escorts behind them. Carlin and the Elves led the way as the Kozaki formed a final rear guard. A distant horn and a great cry went up behind them, but they did not dare turn back to see who prevailed. Instead, they rode toward the Vale.

* * *

All day they rode, and ever the smell of greenery grew stronger. Everywhere they looked were flowering shrubs and green trees, those of the leaf and those of the fruit. Ever they climbed toward the Mountains, and as they did the trees and shrubs grew thicker, closing in upon them. The mists of the Vale rose about them, the thundering river Wyryn lost beneath the clouds as the air grew cooler and moister.

Slowly and steadily they climbed, dismounting at times to give their horses a rest and striding through grasses and plants that rose around their knees. Midday arrived, and the Gracies and their escort broke their fast with food from their saddle bags and fragrant wines supplied by the three Kozaki riders. Then they pushed on, riding ever upwards, determined to reach the Vale before sunset. The last rays of the setting sun shown upon their faces in reds and oranges as they entered the Vale proper, waiting as custom dictated until they were acknowledged by the Magi.

Soon the deep humming song of the Magi appeared all around them, and the Magi appeared, rising from the ground. Priscus was there, his closest friends taking the shapes of stone piles and pillars of water.

'Greetings, my small friends,' said Priscus. 'Never before have your kind journeyed to our home, but you are most welcome. We hear and see that you have come with great tidings for us and for all of the lands.'

Huw asked Priscus that their escort be allowed to enter the Vale and spend the night as they would.

'All may enter, but the Men, valiant though they may be, can only ride to a place prepared for them along the river. There they must stay the night, while you Gracies and the Elves will continue on with me.'

Listening to Huw's request that they follow Priscus' orders, the Kozaki leader, Ivanor, began to protest that the Gracies were still under his protection, but Carlin through Huw was able to reassure him; they exchanged a long look with one another, until the rider said, 'I understand that you will be in no danger here in the Vale. Take all of the time that you need to complete your mission.'

The Gracies and their escort rode forward, but after a hundred yards, Carlin, leading the precious pack horse behind him, noticed a curious hum and buzz coming from the boxes that held the Gemwings.

Keeping their horses to a walk across the valley floor, the Gracies were consumed with awe as they gazed at the wonder about them, the sheer mountain sides rising about them, with the thunder of the falls echoing in a gentle yet loud roar across the vale. Soon they came to a stream, where they left their horses to graze and continued deeper into the Vale. When they reached the great wooden wall, the Gracies were astounded that trees could be so vast, with branches that disappeared into the mists above them.

When they entered the holy grove, the Gracies did not know what to make of the glowing colors filling the center of the grove thirty feet off of the ground. The colors formed an amorphous shape, sometimes a sphere, sometimes a long ellipse, that changed and evolved as the Gracies stared, transfixed. Priscus was silent when suddenly a green light shot from the sphere and touched upon the packs of the Gracies' horses. Distinct and incredibly bright, the light glanced along the packs, and the humming grew louder from the Gemwings, their urgency growing with each passing moment.

As the light from the setting sun faded into a deep dusk, Huw moved to release the Gemwings. Spreading their diamond wings within the green light that covered them, the two great insects took flight. They vanished into the gloaming for several minutes, followed by the green light. A rich pink light emerged from the colored shape, and this light now focused upon the Gracies' packs.

Huw opened his pack, revealing an enormous piece of wood covered with an unusual cluster of small brown spheres like grapes, only slightly smaller, that were held within a substance somewhere between amber and honey. Berwyn, Rolly, and Reggie had seen this odd object briefly in the firelight of their campfire in Platonia, but now guessed it was the Gemwing eggs that Huw had mentioned.

The eggs began to glow, and Huw gently removed them from the pack. A sharp blue light shot from the sphere, guiding Huw to the edge of the grove of ancient trees. A small hollow emerged from the trunk of the most ancient of the trees, and Huw placed the piece of wood with the spheres within this hollow. Immediately, the blue light flickered out, and the Gracies lost sight of Huw as the sphere began to emanate more and more subtle shades of colors. The colors quickly grew too bright to look at directly, forming thin streams of light that were incredibly intense, colored strands that hurtled out from the center of the grove to touch upon the branches of the great trees and moving even higher.

Rapidly the mists of the Vale were consumed and subsumed by the jets of light. The rays, reflecting from their contact points amongst the trees, gained in power instead of losing their luster and became brighter as they emerged from the tops of the trees and touched the sides of the mountains. A gorgeous labyrinth of color was formed, with deep shades of coral pink and salmon, along with hints of saffron, merging into the streams of light. The strands pulsed and danced from point to point, growing in power and intensity as the trees pulled down the magic from the falling waters, transforming it into beams forming within their branches. Focused by the will of the trees, the light emerged with the intensity of many rising suns in the morning from the center of the grove.

Shielding their faces at this most puissant light, the Gracies turned away from the center of the grove, astounded as Huw appeared just visible from the edge of the trees, his eyes shut and his arms outstretched. The brilliant beams faded away as Huw walked forward a few paces toward his friends. A pink light shone forth from the sphere, strong but welcoming, forming a rosy cloud around the eggs of the Gemwings ensconced within the eldest tree. A motion was seen in the light, which seemed to caress the eggs, enveloping them in warmth and protection, exuding even to Berwyn's limited mind a feeling of life and hope, as if the light were begging the eggs to grow and mature. Gentle movement was seen within the eggs, and the first of them opened, revealing a tiny insect emerging from its chrysalis. Suspending itself for several moments along the shell of its incubation, the insect began to pump tiny wings that steadily grew larger and brighter; emitting a tiny glow that challenged yet also complemented the light emanating from the grove. Taking a great leap, the baby Gemwing fell back off its chrysalis. Rotating in mid-fall, it began to flap its wings and flew toward the center of the light.

Huw, who had paused during this blessed event, began walking again toward the center of the grove as the two adult Gemwings swooped down upon him. Purple flames gushed from their faces, burning his clothes away but leaving his body unharmed. Soon Huw was naked. Yet he continued to stride toward the center of the sphere. Suddenly his body was enwrapped by a large pseudopod that extended from the sphere. He rose from the ground, his arms outstretched, his face turned up to the midnight blue sky above him. The light from the spheres changed at that moment, becoming a golden hue like beams of sunlight before dusk truly enters upon the land, encompassing those mortals fortunate enough to see it in that brief time before the colors of orange and red prevail. This night, however, the Gracies were able to see this most fleeting of colors erupt from the center of the grove to glance and shine off the trees and mountainsides in a riot of color. Exploding in intensity, the beams of light formed their own mysterious dance, crossing back and forth in a maze of beams too quick to follow, reflecting up from the center of the groves to the mountainsides. The beams were so intense that they began to melt the stony sides of the granitic cliffs above them, the ice that clung to them vaporized within their glow, adding to the intensity of the beams as they sought the heavens.

Now the heavens responded to the immense power of the lights of the grove. Rain and thunder gathered overhead, exploding in a cacophony of sound. Rain streamed down in torrents, meeting the intense energy of the lights and the molten rock on the mountainside, transforming itself into giant clouds of steam. Lightning bolts lanced downward, mirroring the shafts of light streaming and dancing from above. When one of the bolts met one of the beams, there was an even louder crash, the pressure of the very air forcing the Gracies upon their faces as the power of the blast reverberated throughout the Vale. Vast glowing clouds formed above the trees, descending from the columns of steam rising above the vale, and, touching the trees, the clouds were entwined within the magic of the trees; sheer raw power poured from the branches of the trees, reinforcing the intense bright beams rising from their branches. With one last burst of power, the lights faded into a gentle glow of pink that filled the entire grove, coloring even the vast towers of clouds that lay above them.

'It is done!' cried Priscus. 'The rebirth will occur! May all the gods favor the Gracies from this day forward.'

Huw's body, still suspended within the magic of the sphere, now began to sink back to earth, with the adult Gemwings in close attendance. The light flickered out from the grove, and each of the Gracies was briefly awash in its radiance, filled with the light and joy of the ancient trees, feeling the enormity of the spectacular event, but not knowing what had happened here.

Huw regained consciousness soon after settling to the floor of the grove, his body covered with purple splotches from the flames of the Gemwings. Glancing about himself, Huw saw that he was naked and asked for clothes. The powerful impact of what he had seen of both the present and the future remained with him for the rest of his years, but now he turned back to the Elves and the Gracies and addressed his friends. 'The Gemwings will now be able to continue their race in Nostraterra, helping also to rejuvenate the Emerald Vale!'

'What happened to you?' asked Berwyn. 'How will the Vale be rejuvenated?'

'I was taken within the magic of the grove and blended with the powers within this Vale. Regarding the rejuvenation of the Vale, the images of the Gemwings were not terribly clear. I saw flames and the rebirth of a forest, which makes no sense to me. Perhaps it will later on.'

'Why did the insects'—as Berwyn insisted on calling them—'burn your clothes off? You look like you fell into a giant vat of preserved plums!'

'The Vale and the Gemwings marked me as one of their own. My fate is now tied to theirs, and they and the Magi will now aid us and come if I call them,' replied Huw in an oddly distant voice.

'Huw, are you alright?' asked Rolly. 'You sound as if you are talking from the bottom of a well.'

'Suffice to know I am different than I was! I can feel the pain of the forests falling to the axes of men, and the grasslands being plowed and tilled. But with help, I believe that we can begin to turn the tide.'

'Forests, grasslands…,' spluttered Berwyn. 'What are you talking about?'

Huw glanced at Berwyn, and for a moment the piercing golden lights from the trees came from Huw's eyes, and Berwyn fell backward, shaken. Huw rose to his feet and, stretching out his hands, began a chant of power in a tongue that none of the Gracies knew. But they sensed that something terrible would occur, and as Huw began sinking deeper into his trance, Carlin leapt toward him, murmuring a counter spell in Elvish. Huw's spell was deflected, and the golden light beginning to flicker from his fingertips faltered, sparks drifting to die away on the breeze.

'These are not your enemies,' said Carlin. 'You must learn to differentiate what you have been given from what you received at your original birth. These are your friends. They cannot possibly understand so quickly what has happened to you.'

'Yes, Carlin,' replied Huw after a few moments. 'You are correct, but with these different voices in my mind, I am confused as to what I see and hear, and to how I feel toward others of my kind.'

Carlin replied, 'I know. That is why I will ride with you to Eldora. Along the way, I will teach you to control your new powers. It is a terrible responsibility.'

Huw turned his glance to where his friends were cowering deep in fear, and his anger toward these creatures that went on two legs faded. Instead, a pink glow emanated from his hands. Gently but rapidly expanding outward, it washed his friends in its beneficent glow. Their fear faded quickly, and in its place Berwyn demanded, 'Why are we riding to Eldora and not our homes? We brought the bugs here, didn't we? Our job is done.'

'Not quite,' said Huw.

'What do you mean not quite?'

'The Gemwings must travel back and forth to Platonia to reproduce, and during their other travels they are the eyes and ears of the Magi, gathering knowledge for the Magi. We will take the flowers from the Vale that the Gemwings live upon and plant them strategically along our path toward Eldora and back again to Platonia. This way, the ancient corridors of flowers that allowed the Gemwings to travel will be reinstated, and the Magi can send the Gemwings forth as their eyes into the lands again.'

'But why do we have to go to Eldora? Surely one of the Magi could go in our place?'

'Perhaps, but Men would not interact with a Magi normally; we must go as innocent travelers to see what Men do not want us to see. Priscus is quite concerned about the intentions of the Men of Eldora and needs our help now, not when the plants are established a year or so from now and the Gemwings can travel safely. Recently he met with Prince Alfrahil of Eldora, and while exploring his mind Priscus realized he may be too weak to rule the kingdom of Men after his father dies. Thus he wishes us to get a true sense of Eldora—Eldora as it really is, not as it is seen through the mind of a sheltered and coddled prince like Alfrahil. Priscus will aid us in return, so let's not quarrel but continue to see lands we have only heard of in tales and legends.'

* * *

The next day, Huw took leave of Priscus, asking as he did so for the aid of the Magi in keeping Platonia safe.

'You shall have our aid,' said Priscus. 'Return in a month and we will be ready to help. Further, upon your return, you and your friends will know what has fully transpired here.'

The Gracies and the Elves returned to the Riders of Kozak, who had been waiting for them just inside the Vale. There Huw approached the sergeant. 'We need to get to Eldora as quickly as possible. Do you think it safe to return to Mostyn and get more riders?'

'I do not know,' said Ivanor. 'Let us ride cautiously to the entrance to the Vale. Hopefully we will be safe until then.

'I have been told that creatures of the Vale will escort us to the mouth of the Vale and that we can establish a temporary camp there while you determine if we can return to Mostyn.' said Huw.

When they reached the mouth of the Vale, they met Rupert and his surviving sixteen riders. Much of his face was covered with a bandage, but he was still able to see out of both eyes.

'We won,' he said before Huw could ask questions. 'but barely. Ten, maybe twelve of the enemy got away. We will ride carefully back to Mostyn. There we can make certain that you Gracies make it to wherever you wish to go within our realm.'

'We really need to get going,' argued Berwyn. 'I want to finish our task and go home!'

'How far do you think that you will ride if the Brigands are waiting for you somewhere else on the road ahead?' asked Rupert.

'What makes you think that they will be waiting for us at all?' retorted Berwyn.

Sighing out loud, Rupert glanced at Huw, who rolled his eyes in frustration, gesturing for Rupert to explain. 'These were well-trained Shardan riders who somehow got through our roving cavalry lines and checkpoints, not to mention getting through Eldoran security. They were certainly not sent to attack a random company of Kozaki riders. None of us have any enemies powerful enough to summon this sort of personal attack. That means they were waiting for you, and they may well be waiting for you in the future. Now, we will ride carefully for Mostyn—there will be no more debate about this.'

Chapter Three

Guests of Eldora

Huw and the Gracies traveled swiftly and carefully to Mostyn. King Bernardus was in a seething rage that his valued guests had been attacked and nearly killed within Kozak. He assembled over two thousand riders in well-ordered companies to search out the remaining Brigands and capture them if they could or kill them if they could not. Five full Faris, over five hundred men, were sent to take the Gracies to Titania on a grueling six-day ride. Huw spent much of this time with Carlin, learning a little about the powers entrusted to him by the wondrous entities of the Vale. Carlin had little magic, however, and bade Huw practice carefully, as an Elven wizard such as Nirdan would be much better at instructing him. Despite these limitations, daily and well into the night the two travelers would converse in Elvish; Huw began to learn not only to control and channel his powers, concentrating on healing spells, but to separate the influence of the Gemwings from his own mind.

The day of their arrival at the borders of Eldora dawned gray and humid. Thunder grumbled in the distance as they were greeted by the Eldoran guards, who passed them through with dispatch. The Kozaki escort rode with them all the way to Titania.

As they approached the city, many citizens stared in wonder and cheered the Gracies as they rode across Sisera. At the gate to the city, their Kozaki escort took their leave and the Gracies thanked them profusely for their help. They were joined by an escort of a hundred mounted men, led by Prince Alfrahil. Alfrahil hailed them as the descendants of the heroes of the Great War and led them into the city. The Gracies amazed at the size of the city and the numbers of people who lined the great road to the Citadel and cheered them joyously, began to feel safe for the first time since they had left their homes to look for the Gemwings.

Carlin and the other Elves were directed to their own quarters while the Gracies were shown to luxurious quarters in the Second District of the city. All of them whistled softly in appreciation at the suite of apartments set out for their stay. A large common room with a dining table and chairs was the center of their accommodations, with a washing chamber and four separate bedrooms and a small kitchen completing their quarters. The furniture was a blend of intricate hardwood and silk coverings for their chairs. Fine white linen was on the table, and incredibly soft cotton sheets were on their beds.

'Well, this is certainly something Huw, isn't it?' asked Berwyn. 'Have you ever seen the like before?'

'Only in the royal quarters in Phoenicia; my room as a junior student was unremarkable. Let us have a wash and tell the guard outside that we are ready to see the king.'

Coming before the king, Huw saw that Creon had a look of weary greatness about him, as if the mantle he wore was wearing thin after all these years. The king invited them, and their Elven escort, to a hastily arranged feast in the royal dining room. They were flattered to sit at the king's table, halfway down the right side, alongside Carlin and the Elves. After the meal, Creon asked for news of their lands, and Huw told him of the brigand attacks on Platonia and against them personally.

Creon was outwardly surprised to hear of the attack upon Platonia and even more astounded to hear of the attack within the heart of Kozak. He conversed briefly with Mergin, who sat to his left. Then orders were hastily written and sent out before the king returned to speaking to his guests.

'These are grave tidings,' said the king. 'That the will of Eldora has been openly thwarted by these wastrels and vagabonds sits ill with me. There is much to learn and much to consider. Mergin, please make the necessary inquiries so I can have all of the information I need.'

'Yes, Sire,' replied Mergin with a groan as he shifted uncomfortably in his chair. Huw could tell the man was in great pain, despite his chair being piled with large cushions.

Coming out of his dark reverie, Creon said, 'You Gracies are more than welcome. While the years may have passed, we do not forget the valiant deeds of your ancestors. The gift of my father shall be upheld, and you and your little land shall be protected against these vile encroachers. You shall return to your homes safe in the knowledge that Eldora will honor its promises.'

Huw rose and bowed, gesturing to the rest of the Gracies to follow his lead, and said, 'We thank you, King Creon, for your generosity, and we pledge our eternal loyalty and gratitude to the realm of Eldora.'

Creon acknowledged this polite but still meaningful gesture with the first genuine smile of the evening, and much of his mood was lightened by his miniature guests and their unabashed joy in their lives. Extending his mind, he focused on each of the Gracies in turn, but very subtly, not with a sudden assault that they would feel. Besides, a full mental bombardment might cause the little folk to collapse out of their chairs. The first three Gracies were hardly remarkable, their minds full of images of the Vale he did not quite understand, but Creon sensed that a great magical event had occurred there that was significant for both the Gracies and the Magi. As he glanced at Huw, however, his mind was rebuffed and directed elsewhere. Creon was astonished, for no one besides Daerahil or Elves could even notice this sort of questioning, must less actively resist it. Focusing his mind harder on Huw, he felt the Gracie's mind become stronger. Huw glanced at him from his chair with a suspicious look, slightly shaking his head. With that Creon, went back to the other Gracies, determined to get specific information that his first casual search had not revealed.

This time, however, his contact with the other Gracies was weak and unclear, the images diluted. He found nothing new. Quietly enraged, he suspected that Huw was protecting them from his inquiries.

'Well, the gloves are off now,' thought Creon, and he let loose a psychic blast that should render Huw unable to protect himself if not knock him unconscious. But he felt his power bounce off of Huw's mind like a small stone off a brick wall. Deflected, this mental assault found the senior minister of Health instead. The poor man let out a screech and collapsed shrieking to the floor next to his chair. The commotion brought Creon's searching to an end; he was forced to direct the aid of his minister and still retain some semblance of a welcoming atmosphere for the dinner party. Yet his mighty mind kept thinking again and again of Huw, and he wondered at the powers that he felt hidden there, powers not endemic to Gracies, unknown to Creon, and for now impenetrable.

The rest of the feast was consumed by eating and drinking, with the king and his son playing the benevolent hosts very well. Huw saw strange men in subdued garb just behind the king, who looked like guardians of some sort, though their faces were covered with dark masks; so it was that the Gracies looked upon the Shadows, though they did not know their name or their capabilities, for the first time, and Huw wondered as to their nature and purpose.

The next day, rising in time for an informal breakfast with a Citadel guard captain, they enjoyed fresh tropical fruits shipped up from Shardan, along with eggs and cereal. Tasting the juice of oranges was a first for all of them, and they dreamed of taking seeds home until they were told that orange trees could not survive a cold northern winter.

After breakfast, they were taken round Titania, even to the top of the tower of Anicetus to see the city in its beauty. An excursion then took them to Ackerlea and part way up the Pestilent Road so they could see the fell city of Malius. Shuddering at the memory of that city of ancient nightmares, Huw could only wonder what it must have been like for his great grandfather, Bran, weak and weary, to pass its baleful hidden eyes at the height of the power of Magnar. Not for the first time did Huw think about the Walkers and wonder if he could measure up to them in any significant way.

The Gracies were journeying back from the Crossroads where they had spent the previous night when they met a company of Lesser Elves heading from Estellius back to the toxic city, looking both weary and ethereal. The morning sun was warm, lighting the Elves from behind, and, seeing a surprising look of disapproval on Carlin's face, Huw knew it was up to him to speak with the Lesser Elves.

Calling to them in the Greater Elven tongue, Huw bid them greetings, but only received blank expressions as their horses trotted toward them, but the Elves replied to the Gracies in the common tongue. The riders immediately turned their horses and rode parallel to the Gracies on the backs of the great horses of Eldora.

'Hail, and well met,' said the leader of the company. 'Felorad am I. May I presume you are each descendants of the four Gracies who participated in the Great War?'

'Yes,' said Huw. 'How did you know?'

'Who else but descendants of the Walkers would leave your refuge of Platonia?' asked Felorad with a smile. 'Besides, rumor of your arrival, along with your names and lineage, has spread like wildfire ever since you entered the realm of Eldora.'

'Are you one of the Elven riders who escorted our ancestors to Plaga Erebus?' asked Huw.

'Alas, I am not, but the Elven Prince of the North Forest, Lord Ferox, is the King's nephew, and he rode with your ancestors,' replied Felorad.

'This is a happy meeting then,' said Huw, introducing the rest of the Gracies and the Elves. He looked at Carlin, but the Greater Elves refused to make eye contact with Felorad. 'These are my escort,' he said indicating Carlin and his Greater Elven companions.

'Yes, I can see that, and also that they do not wish to speak with us,' said Felorad. 'Perhaps another time they will be friendly. We no longer speak the Greater Elven tongue in our land of the North Forest, as Lord Ferox forbids all who look to him as liege lord from doing so.'

Huw wondered at this obvious antipathy between Felorad and the Greater Elves, but knew that now was not the time or place to ask awkward questions.

'Do you have time to journey to our city of the Elves here in Ackerlea?' asked Felorad. 'My Lord Prince would be happy to meet with such famous Gracies.'

'Alas,' said the Eldoran captain, 'they depart in a few days. They are already overdue for their journey to see the river districts, and then they must be on their way home.'

'I find it curious you could journey so far from your homes and be leaving so soon,' said Felorad.

'Well, we could stay longer, but we have to return to the Vale,' burst out Rolly. 'He expects us back in a fortnight.'

'Quiet,' hissed Huw. 'Actually, my companion is overcome with last night's wine and this morning's bright sun. What he means is that we must return to our home via the river vales. Business will not wait.'

'Well,' answered Felorad with another smile, 'I hope you will be able to return someday soon to enjoy the hospitality of the Elves of Ackerlea. We heard rumor of you and your travels just a few days ago; we have prepared these small gifts as a remembrance of your ancestors' great help in defeating the Shadow of Plaga Erebus.'

Extending his hand, Felorad was given four identical bundles wrapped in silk by one of his escort. Felorad handed each of the Gracies one of the bundles, and Berwyn opened his bundle first. Berwyn first pulled out a corselet of fine Elven armor light enough to wear daily yet tough enough to defeat any blade not made by an Elf or a Dwarf, along with a cloak that seemed to shimmer with many colors. A box of flower and tree seeds was also included, along with a necklace of small bright crystals.

'Take these as gestures of our good will; we see you are wearing no armor, and in these uncertain times you might find yourself under attack, not only by Men who covet what you have, but by others who wish to stop you from your traveling. Plant the seeds within your land and receive the blessing of the Elves of the woods.'

Accepting these marvelous gifts, the Gracies thanked the Elves profusely.

'Say nothing of it,' said Felorad. 'It is the least we can do for you. Please return when you can and stay as long as you like in our realm. Safe journey.'

Huw raised his hand in salute to Felorad, and, with a flourish, the salute was returned. The two groups then went their separate ways. As the Gracies rode swiftly back toward the bridge, Huw said, 'Well, I must say, it was very generous of them to equip us.'

'Indeed,' said Reggie. 'Now maybe you can spend some time researching this new armor and these extraordinary Elven cloaks. Surely we can use them to aid our people.'

* * *

Felorad paused with his troop and smiled after the Gracies, but his chief companion said, 'It was unwise to give them our mail, much less our cloaks. You heard their High Elven speech. Perhaps the 'Ghost of Elvalon,' as we call Emedius, will examine our newer mail and old cloaks, learning their secrets. We will then have lost part of our advantage.'

'Nonsense,' said Felorad. 'Emedius was severely wounded helping the Gracies escape from their little land and may not survive even in Phoenicia. The cloaks we gave them were recently altered in the Elven city and were brought specifically for the Gracies.'

'If Emedius recovers, he may uncover the secrets of our cloaks and mail,' persisted the other Elf.

'What if he does? It will only reinforce their arrogance that only the Great Elves can truly make armor that would repel all blades. Besides, to Elven eyes the cloaks can be seen for miles,' said Felorad.

'Why do we want to be able to see them?' asked the other Elf.

'Four Gracies suddenly appearing in Eldora on a holiday?' snorted Felorad. 'I think not. They are here to ask for something or to look for something, but what it is I do not know.'

'What did they mean by 'Vale'¿asked his companion. 'Perhaps something to do with the Magi and their realm?'

'Perhaps,' said Felorad. 'That puzzles me the most. Why, but perhaps for curiosity, would the Gracies want to see the Magi, and why would the Magi want to see them? Good thing we can send someone to look after them and not be seen!'

* * *

Two days later, the Gracies were taken by boat from Estellius downriver just above the great Swamp, where the river widened and the current slowed to a nearly imperceptible pace. Mosquitoes and other biting insects were blown upon the breeze, annoying the Gracies, but the wind also carried sea gulls far inland, calling in their tongues, and the Gracies' hearts were moved, as all creatures are who stand by the sea.

Berwyn contented himself with wandering up to the rail of the great ship and looking at the mighty flow of the Aphon. Today the wind had failed them, and draft horses were slowly pulling the boat up against the stream, aided by slaves shackled below the decks.

'Who are the men chained to the oars?' asked Huw.

'They are criminals who repeatedly defy the king's peace and his authority; their punishment is to occupy the rowing decks on the king's ships until their sentences are concluded,' responded the escort captain.

'How long are their sentences?' asked Rolly.

'That depends,' replied the captain. 'The men in the front of the boats usually spend less than a year here, the others longer, and some all of their natural lives. It depends what law they broke, their law-breaking history, or if they upset the king personally.'

'And how much money they and their families can raise for the chief warden of the jails,' said one of the sailors.

'Peace,' said the captain with a flash of angry eyes. 'Do not insult our guests with your fanciful tales.'

'Tales?' replied the sailor, as if not seeing the look or hearing the tone in the captain's voice. 'Just telling them the truth, that's all. When my cousin was arrested for assault, he was given six months of hard rowing, but a little gold in the right places got him out in two weeks, and he was back to running his joy house before you could whistle a tune.'

'But even gold can't save you, if the King hates you, just look at what happened to Prince Daerahil.' interjected another sailor.

'Daerahil, who is he?' asked Huw.

'A Prince on special assignment by the king, but please give me a moment and admire the river view.'

Forestalling the Gracies' other questions, the captain dragged the oafish sailor off and had a few choice words with him.

'So it seems,' said Huw, 'that the nobility of Eldora and its pure image are a bit tarnished after all.'

'Well, you don't think the gaming houses sprang up in Alton by themselves, do you?' asked Berwyn.

Huw responded in the hand speech. 'No, you are quite correct. There is much more here than meets the ear or eye. Let us ask questions, but say little of ourselves and our journey, only that we were concerned about the Brigands. I do not trust this king or his politics, despite his fair words.'

Later, when Berwyn, impolitic as usual, asked about Daerahil at the parting feast held in the Gracies' honor, Lord Mergin replied in a dark and forbidding tone. 'He is leading the new expedition to Plaga Erebus, very important work and a prestigious posting.'

One counselor seated at the high table in the royal dining room was unable to stifle a chuckle at this pronouncement.

'Do you have anything to say?' demanded Mergin.

'No, Lord Mergin, forgive my lapse,' said the frightened counselor, returning to his repast.

One of the chief servers managed to walk briefly with Huw as he was returning from the washroom down the hall and whispered that if he would like to see the kitchens and get some cooking instruction, to follow him. Standing and not taking his seat after returning from the washroom, Huw asked the king, 'May we be excused to the kitchens to see these wonderful cooks at work?'

Surprise flitted across Creon's face, but the king replied, 'Certainly, but please return before the toast of parting.'

The king granted his permission to leave the feast, though court protocol demanded that no one leave the table until the king finished his meal. After the Gracies left, Mergin muttered this quietly to the king, and Creon replied softly, 'We must make allowances for the rustic little folk. They can come to little mischief in the kitchens. Besides, the Shadow that follows them around the city may be able to find out more of their travel to the Vale and what happened there.'

'Are you still not able to penetrate the little folk's thoughts?'

'No, and this continues to confound me. I can get general feelings from all of the Gracies except for their leader, Huw, but his mind remains indomitable by mine. He was given tremendously powerful gifts, I suspect, by Priscus and the Magi, the nature of which, and why they were given to him, I do not know. Subterfuge and stealth must be our tools to uncover what they know and what they plan to do.'

The other Gracies happily rose to their feet, eager to see the great kitchens that would interest any hungry Gracie's heart.

Entering the kitchens, Huw knew that Berwyn, Reggie, and Rolly were enjoying themselves and would keep any watchers busy for a minute. Catching a glimpse of something out of the corner of his eye, Huw was sure there was someone following them. The server brought one of the master chefs from the kitchen and introduced the Gracies. Berwyn said excitedly, 'I would love to learn how you prepared that fish with the crème sauce tonight.'

'Certainly little master if it's for your kitchen up north,' replied the chef. 'It is a well-guarded secret here. Come let us go to the preparation kitchens. It is quieter there.'

Chattering away, Berwyn, Reggie, and Rolly walked with the chef into the front kitchen, while Huw waited till they were out of earshot. Catching his eye, the accompanying server gave the faintest of nods. 'This way, young master, and you will be able to see the great fry pans.'

A cavernous room was before him. The roar of the flames and the hiss of the cooking food made a great cacophony of noise in the flickering yellow light. Here, great iron pans three feet in diameter were set above banks of charcoal on metal racks. Some of the charcoal fires glowed nearly white hot, searing the food placed within the great pans rapidly, while other fires looked nearly dormant, with only a faint dark red glimmer telling of the gentle but steady heat they gave off. There were various degrees of heat from several different fires, allowing food to be cooked simultaneously at the required temperatures. Huw could see the pans had great eye hooks on the sides and were hung by chains from pulleys above them. The entire arrangement was designed so that the pans could be pushed and pulled rapidly over the different fires; with the long chains ensuring the heat from below was distributed evenly and would allow the dishes to be cooked perfectly and quickly for the king's banquets. Huw looked up and saw there were other chefs in heavy clothing standing on a walkway above the pans and stirring the food with long paddles. Long tongs, nearly ten feet in length, were in one man's hands, and Huw could see what looked like a whole filet of beef being expertly turned within its pan. Other chefs sent down gestures to the journeyman cooks to transfer the pans from different fires, or to remove them from the heat altogether for service to the tables.

Gesturing as if explaining the subtleties of the methods amongst the roaring flames and sizzling fires from the pans, the server said in a voice just loud enough for Huw to hear, 'Keep looking at where I am pointing, and listen carefully to what I say. My name is Andor; Prince Daerahil is in exile for defying the king's will and for assaulting the king's first minister. What you don't know is that the prince has heard about the troubles you are having with the squatters adjacent to your lands, and he is sympathetic about removing them permanently. He asks that you look for nearby lands where they would be welcome and send word to me here at the kitchens, care of Andor. I will make certain Prince Daerahil receives it.

'Keep these thoughts to yourself,' Andor continued. 'Do not discuss them even with your traveling companions. You were right to look over your shoulder on your way in here with me. The cloaked and hooded men standing behind the king are called Shadows. They are scouts, messengers, and assassins, and they are utterly loyal to the king and his first minister. He is clearly determined to keep an eye on you and your companions while you are here. I suspect there will be at least one Shadow who will follow you home to spy on you, and perhaps more, as they generally travel in groups of three. Beware—they are difficult to see and deadly if provoked. Let them see nothing unusual about the rest of your visit, and you will be fine. Take care in talking until you return home, as I fear your land will be under watch now, with these tidings.'

'How do I know you speak the truth, for your name merely means 'gift' in your tongue.'

Andor replied, 'My true name is unimportant, but I am a loyal supporter of Prince Daerahil. The king and his ministers know nothing of me. Regarding my veracity, why would I lie to you and your friends? Clearly you have seen that what is said and what is done are two different things in Eldora. Believe me or not, but I suspect you will see the truth of my words. Now, say nothing to anyone, including your friends, about our conversation here. We have tarried enough—let us talk only of food and of the pastry rooms we are about to see, and remember to keep quiet.'

'How do you know that I can be trusted?' insisted Huw.

'I do not know that you can be trusted,' replied Andor. 'But unless you have the desire to see my body screaming over one of Mergin's torture pits, say nothing to anyone until you are far away from Eldora.'

The Gracies, now joined by Huw, spent the next hour examining the preparation rooms and greedily absorbing the techniques from the pastry rooms. 'Folding pastry dough,' said Reggie. 'Who would ever have imagined it?'

'Yes,' said one of the chefs, 'but it must be kept very cold, or the butter will melt and ruin the pastry. We are only able to make it with the ice that is collected and stored during the winter months. Here is an easier, simpler recipe that you can make without the need for ice, though it is not nearly as spectacular as the folded pastry.' He handed Reggie a small folded parchment.

The Gracies returned to the feast table in time for the parting toast to the king's health. Reggie, Rolly, and Berwyn had their minds full of the fantastic cooking methods they had observed in their foray into the kitchens, but Huw reflected upon his meeting with Andor.

The next day in the courtyard of the Citadel, so early that the walls cast long shadows over the Gracies, the king gave them a rousing speech and pledged the protection of Eldora to Platonia and hailed the four Gracies for the ancient bravery of their forefathers and their desire to renew ties with Eldora. Adding many praises to the Great Elves as well, Creon saw Carlin nod gently to the king's compliments, before turning his horse and leading his Elves out of the city, destined for Phoenicia.

The Gracies were then escorted by knights of Eldora, who would take them to borders of Kozak where they would be taken to the edge of the horse kingdom and once outside Kozak, they would be escorted by Eldoran cavalry from Amadeus to return home to Platonia. The king said, 'The guard stations have been notified of your coming and are instructed to offer you every courtesy. An armed company will keep you safe until you are no longer in the lands of Eldora.'

Thanking the king in the common tongue, Huw added, in the ancient speech of Nostraterra, 'May the light of the west continue to shine on this land and her king, and may our next meeting be soon and joyous.'

Prince Alfrahil responded in the ancient tongue, saying, 'May the light of the west shine on your journey so you shall reach home safely. Tarry not long before we see you again.'

Taking leave of Carlin and their Elven escort, the Gracies mounted horses and moved towards the city gate.

* * *

Creon, Alfrahil, and Mergin met briefly in the Council chamber after the Gracies were safely on their way out of the city.

'It disturbs me that these landless men would dare to attack Platonia openly,' said the king. 'Things are not well in Amadeus. Frederic does not appear able to control what goes on in his own kingdom. If he cannot control men in his own kingdom, how can we expect him to pacify Shardan and follow our wishes?'

'Clearly Frederic has fallen into the same malaise that pervades much of Eldora and Amadeus,' said Alfrahil. 'If we send Daerahil north after his exile in Plaga Erebus is over, we can put him in charge of transforming Amadeus into a more virtuous realm.'

'How can you say that,' demanded Mergin, 'after the events he has caused here, including assaulting me? Even now we are tracing the links of corruption throughout all of Eldora, and I am certain he is at the bottom of this mess.'

'Yes, Lord Mergin,' rejoined Alfrahil vehemently. 'But you have had nearly four full months, and despite the arrests and confessions that you have already obtained, we have no firm connections between my brother and the corruption. He consorts with these men, surely, and they entertain him with feasts and wine, but no houses or monies have been transferred to him from these men that we can find. I suspect neglect of his administration duties is the truth rather than actual participation in graft and greed. Besides, the more important aspect has always been to discover who was behind the assassination attempts upon me. Why have they stopped? What have we learned since my brother's trial? I will answer you, Lord Mergin: nearly nothing.'

Mergin began to speak heatedly, but the king said, 'You may be correct, my son. Perhaps if we send him north after his tour in Plaga Erebus is finished, he can indeed begin removing the local corruption in Amadeus. My one concern is that he may not be willing to discipline these invaders who are attacking our little friends in Platonia.'

'The King of Kozak seems more than willing to safeguard their borders, and he is no friend to Daerahil,' said Mergin after some moments of reflection. 'Let the Kozaki continue to protect the little land of Platonia, and we will give Daerahil instructions to clean up the gambling dens and halls of vice in Amadeus. If he fails, or refuses to restore order in Amadeus, then he can be exiled again and for a longer period of time. This will both isolate him from his friends here in Eldora and deny him access to his Shardan veterans and potential traitorous allies.'

'Perhaps there is merit in both suggestions. However, I am confused, Lord Mergin, that you have suddenly changed your mind about Daerahil. Why is that?'

'Sire, I have had time to put aside my anger at your son's cowardly assault on me, and I am only concerned for the safety of the realm,' said Mergin, deflecting the king's question.

Alfrahil was suddenly very suspicious of Mergin and his rapid change in heart. Extending his newfound emotional powers to Mergin, he sensed only a dark hatred toward Daerahil, with duplicity and false sincerity intertwining his thoughts. Alfrahil said nothing at this time, unsure when and if he could reveal his findings to his father without betraying the trust of the Magi.

Mergin then said, 'Meanwhile. I will send three Shadows north to watch the little people and see what mischief and machinations they might be up to. They can also explore the borders of Platonia and come back via Amadeus, giving us a better sense as to what is really occurring in the lands of the north kingdom. I would suggest Frederic remain in Amadeus so that the Shadows can fully explore his corruption until Daerahil arrives there. Not only would this give Daerahil information that he might find useful, but leaving a void by bringing Frederic south now would not be advisable. Who knows what could happen without a royal prince to govern the kingdom, no matter how ineptly? Once the Shadows have been able to investigate Frederic, then Daerahil can be sent north.'

'Very well,' said the king. 'Make it so. Is there anything else that we need to discuss now?'

Alfrahil nodded. 'Father, the scouts are beginning to return from their expedition. I should make ready to ride to meet them at the rendezvous, for they may have many interesting things to tell us, perhaps even news that can help us track down the source of the corruption and the attempts on my life.'

'Make yourself ready, my son,' said the king. 'Take Shadows with you as we have discussed and keep this meeting only between ourselves—no one else needs to know.'

Bowing, both Mergin and Alfrahil left the king's presence, each going about his separate tasks.

Chapter Four

The Tempest of the Trees

Departing the city, the Gracies ignored the wind and rain dampening during their journey as each night they enjoyed luxurious accommodations. 'This is traveling in style,' said Berwyn the first night to general agreement as they lay in silk sheets and soft wool blankets on traveling cots under the roof of a rigid shelter instead of a leaky tent.

When they arrived at the Kozaki border, they were turned over to the care of the Kozaki riders, who escorted them directly to Mostyn and the great hall of Halen, mostly empty except for a few feasting nobles and bankers. King Bernardus was gone, they heard, looking for more rumors of the Dark Elves, but his first minister extended the king's hospitality in his absence and asked after their needs.

'We will begin our journey to our homes on the morrow,' Huw answered, 'but we will return to the Vale first, prior to leaving for our lands.'

The minister replied with a curious smile, 'Five Faris of riders, led by your friend Rupert, will escort you to and from the Vale and back to Mostyn and then as far as the borders of Kozak, and see you safely on your way to the first guard station of Eldora.'

Thanking him, the Gracies retired early and were up just after dawn, looking forward to a relaxing journey to the Vale rather than their initial mad dash. Five days later they arrived at the Vale without mishap; nevertheless, Huw thought he saw a figure at a slight distance constantly dogging their footsteps. Using his powers as innocuously as possible, he was able to feel a Man, perhaps two, keeping an eye on them, most likely Shadows.

When they arrived at the Vale, Rupert led twenty riders as escort, the others remaining encamped below: They rode ever upwards, clouds of mist rose and fell in the golden colors of early afternoon, serving as a beacon. Approaching the Vale proper, they waited with their Kozaki escort for permission to enter. Soon Priscus was seen approaching from the north rim of the valley. Two other Magi were present as well.

'Well, my little friends,' said Priscus, 'you are several days late, but perhaps that was good. Our preparations took longer than I thought they would.'

'Indeed,' said Huw. 'May we enter into the Vale, and may our escort have leave to spend the night encamped here?'

'Certainly you may enter,' said Priscus. 'There is much to show you, and so long as these Men do no damage, they are welcome here.'

After walking half a mile or so, Huw asked, 'Can we withdraw to a quieter place? There is much to tell you.'

'Quieter?' asked Priscus. 'There are only ourselves and my two Magi friends here; you look as if you are troubled.'

'Please,' repeated Huw. 'Let us adjourn to a quieter place, and could you have the Vespre escort us there and keep all but us from going there?'

'Certainly,' said Priscus. A graver expression shone in his eyes, and he gave forth a great booming cry that ended in a breathy sigh. The two other Magi rapidly moved, one to the entrance of the Vale to keep an eye on the men of Kozak, and the other deeper into the Vale, toward the Holy Grove. Soon a misty series of shadows, of trees and darkness, began to emerge from the sides of the Vale. Rapidly encircling the Gracies and Priscus, the Vespre formed a moving circle that drifted inward toward them.

As they entered the glade, Huw felt a surge of anger from the Vespre, and their sighing speech rapidly increased in volume. A sudden motion amongst them and the grunting sounds of a struggling Man were heard from the circle. Priscus bade the Gracies remain still. Passing to the edge of the circle, he whispered and sighed with the Vespre, and soon a masked Man in grubby clothes designed to mimic the woods and grasses was dropped in front of Priscus. Moving too quickly for the Gracies to see, Priscus picked the man up in a great fist and held him by the waist fifteen feet off the ground so he was at eye level with Priscus.

'Who are you? Why have you come to our valley?' asked Priscus.

'I am a messenger of Eldora. I will not answer to you or anyone but the king,' replied the man.

'He does not tell the truth,' said Huw. 'He is a Shadow.'

'What is a Shadow as to other Men?' asked Priscus of Huw.

'They are spies and possibly assassins in the direct employ of the King of Eldora and his ministers. Why he is here, I do not know.'

'Did you know he was following you?' asked Priscus.

'I suspected we were followed,' said Huw. 'But I was warned by someone in Eldora that this might happen and we should be wary of our speech. That is why I had you bring us here.'

'Well, does he speak the truth, messenger?' asked Priscus contemptuously. 'Are you a Shadow as my good friend names you? Are you a spy?'

'I am a messenger of the king,' replied the Shadow. 'Release me immediately or you will know the king's wrath.'

'I think not,' said Priscus, reaching out and removing the man's mask. Dark hair and pale skin were revealed in a face that was both old and young. 'One last chance to tell me willingly,' said Priscus, 'or I will force this information from your mind. The pain will be terrible, and you may not recover.'

'You do not frighten me,' said the man.

A greenish glow began to surround Priscus, and thin wisps of mist appeared, touching the face of the Shadow. Huw watched the Shadow restrain most of his first scream, but Huw suspected that the Shadow knew he could not resist this assault for long. The Shadow then moved his left hand in a blur toward his face. A small spring-mounted blade stabbed out from the sleeve of his tunic, impaling his own throat. A gurgling sound was heard, and the Gracies averted their eyes as the Shadow's body hit the ground with a thud. The Vespre swirled about them in a cloud, taking the Shadow's body away.

Muttering darkly, Priscus said, 'I have never seen a Man, Dwarf, or Elf act so strangely before.'

'How did he get past the Vespre is what I would like to know,' demanded Berwyn.

'The Vespre have a difficult time distinguishing between mortals.' responded Priscus. 'As you and the Kozaki had our permission to be here, they did not differentiate between you Gracies, the Kozaki, and this other man. I had them keep their distance, as I did not need them to keep a close watch on welcome guests. I will maintain a constant watch of Vespre to secure the Vale from tonight forward.'

Not knowing what to say, Berwyn muttered under his breath.

Priscus bade the Gracies enter the Holy Grove and see for themselves the re-birth that Priscus had spoken of during their first visit. Within the great ring of ancient trees, the Gracies noted immediately that there were small trees grow-ing at the roots of their forefathers. Too small be called saplings, they were mere green shoots, but of the same color, glowing faintly in the light from the spheres.

'Now you shall see a secret known only to the Magi before this day,' said Priscus. 'Even the Greater Elves have not been given this secret.'

Gesturing to Huw, Priscus retreated from the center of the grove as Huw lifted his arms and hands before him, using the chant of summoning given to him by the Bubblers in Platonia when he became chief acolyte.

As Huw sang in a high-pitched tone that changed in frequency and rhythm quickly, his arms began to glow with a familiar pink light. The light gently emanated out from his fingertips. Hints of emerald green were mixed in with the pink glow. A small cloud of Gemwings appeared around them, their tiny bodies flitting and darting all around the Gracies and Elves, multiple colored flames emerging as bright sparks from their mouths. Suddenly their parents swooped down from above, and, after hovering for a few moments in front of Huw, they flew upward to the lowest branches of the great trees above them.

The light grew in intensity from Huw, and now a bright sapphire light emerged from the branches of the tree, illuminating great seed pods that hung from the branches. The Gemwings flew in tandem in perfect opposition around the periphery of a circle that they created. Now the same purple flames that had burned away Huw's clothes a month ago flickered out, touching a seed pod. Round and round the Gemwings circled. The scent of the melting resins contained within the pod filled the noses of the Gracies with an unknown fra-grance. Deep musky hints brought forth images of the earth, while a sharp and crisp hint of cold air suddenly reminded them of air on a clear winter's morning. Sulfur and wood smoke dredged memories of autumnal fires, which gave way to the odors of marshes and rushes along the riverbanks of clean water. As the resin melted and dripped, Priscus placed a small crystal bowl underneath the seed pod to catch this mysterious liquid.

Over all the odors of living earth and growing plants were present, when suddenly the seed pod exploded with a sharp pop, and a small sphere of all the colors of the rainbow fell from the charred pod. Darting below the shriveled pod, one of the Gemwings took the seed to a place on the floor of the vale, adjacent to one of the great trees, as a patch of blue light emanated from the closest tree, indicating the precise spot. The Gemwing parents then rapidly dug a shallow hole, burying the seed within the soil. Their task complete, the Gemwings flew back up into the arboreal canopy. Then the tree above them moved its branches through the deep mist, and soon a small trickle of water was directed by its branches onto the spot where the seed had gone into the earth. Many minutes passed, but a tiny shoot rose from the ground, no more than a blade of grass. Then Huw put his hands down, and the glow from his limbs faded, and he gently collapsed upon the soft ground. Priscus tended to the small crystal bowl briefly; a flare of light came from his hands, and he set the bowl onto the ground.

'Now, my young friends, you have seen what no other has ever seen in Nostraterra: the rebirth of the Cloud Trees,' said Priscus. 'These trees must have the magic fire of the Gemwings to dissolve the protective coatings of the seeds, allowing them to germinate, completing the cycle of life here in the Vale.'

Marveling at the sight and not knowing what to say, the Gracies were happy when Huw awoke from his swoon and began to explain.

'The Gemwings will remain here in the Vale until the flowers they feed upon are replanted at regular intervals along their migration routes,' he said. 'The only people they trust to perform this task are we Gracies.'

'What were you doing just now?' asked Berwyn.

'The Bubblers taught me an ancient charm of summoning, something they teach each chief acolyte in case it is needed. Now we have the aid that we will need to restore the Well of Life.'

'What aid, and why did they not do this the first time we were here?'

'The Gemwings and Priscus needed time to determine how they could help us recharge the Well, so that the Bubblers can be renewed, but they still needed my participation. You do remember that's why we set out on this journey in the first place?'

'What help?' persisted Berwyn.

'Look in the crystal bowl and you will find your answer.'

Inside the bowl were several brown ovoids that gave off the same intoxicating scent that the seed pod had as it melted.

'These will renew our Well,' said Huw. 'The Gemwings tell me the effect will last at least a year or so per pod, plenty of time for the plants that we will take with us to take root and bloom, forming an initial pathway to Platonia for the Gemwings to leave the Vale. It took Priscus and the others a great deal of thought as to how to transform the resin of the seed pods into a solid form of magic that would heal our Well and also dissolve in water. Now, I don't know about you, but I am exhausted and need to sleep.'

Their minds swirling with what they had learned, the Gracies laid themselves down to sleep, content that their part in these great events was over.

The following day, the Gracies prepared to leave the Vale, anxious to return to their homes, concerned that the Brigands might have caused terrible destruction prior to the arrival of the Kozaki riders.

Priscus approached them and said, 'I am happy to tell you that the most vulnerable of our Cloud trees has new shoots growing to replace her. We no longer have to concentrate all of our powers keeping her alive. The circle of the Grove will remain intact, and since the trees are the source of our powers, we will be able to remain here in the Vale. In fact, one of us will escort you home to protect Platonia and instruct you in planting the flowers along the way for the Gemwings. The Magi called Eolus shall go with you north, and he will travel with a group of Vespre as well; they will keep you and Platonia safe in days ahead. Once you finish planting the flower seeds for the Gemwings, the pathway back and forth from the Vale to Platonia will be restored; the Gemwings will restore your Well every year.

'You should now rejoin your escort,' said Priscus, 'and ride down the valley on your way home. Once you are on the road home, and outside the presence of Men, Eolus will come to you and speak with you more about your journey. Farewell, my young Gracies! You have honored the request and trust placed upon you by the Gemwings beyond any hope.'

Taking their leave, the Gracies moved across the Vale to the entrance where their escort was waiting with their horses. Riding down the valley toward the bridge over the great river, the Gracies were quiet and subdued, overwhelmed with the tremendous events in the Vale.

Eolus introduced himself briefly before disappearing ahead of the Gracies with a small cloud of mist hanging close to the ground: the only evidence that Vespre were with him, heading for Platonia.

Thirteen days later, having taken the time to plant the flowers of the Gemwings in certain clearings along their route, the Gracies paused for nuncheon, sitting upon the border between the plains of Kozak and the Eldoran kingdom of Amadeus. The Gracies and their Kozaki escort had ridden steadily, with Eolus and the Vespre nowhere to be seen. Huw had snuck away at night on occasion, using his powers to hide from the Kozaki patrols, to seek instructions from Eolus. Now the grassy track in Kozak gave way to a stone road again, the continuation of the great northwest road that would take them to Platonia. The road forked a narrow segment heading westward toward the Southwest Highlands, bending south to avoid the dark forest, at the only natural fords of the Beadle River at Barhart. The main stone road traveled northward into the kingdom of Amadeus, and Huw knew that they would follow this road for a while.

Their Kozaki escort bade them farewell, having received reports from southbound riders that the brigands had been slain or chased northward into the Never Summer Range. The riders had also encouraged the squatters who had built their rude farms adjacent to the Beadle to move elsewhere. The only unusual sign the riders had seen or heard was a distant terrible sound, a sound so deep it made their horses uneasy, but when they went to look for the source, they found nothing, just distant echoes that made the soldiers uneasy as well. Without a discernible threat, the riders entrusted a company of Eldoran soldiers to see them to the fords of Platonia.

Thanking the Kozaki riders for all of their help, the Gracies saddled up their horses and began the last leg of their journey.

Reaching Barhart late on a gray afternoon that threatened rain before nightfall, the Gracies put up for the night at a local inn. Settling onto chairs of Men, they required cushions so they could reach the table. Having bypassed this town in their rapid passage through the lands, they were looked at with wonder, but the king's orders had run before them and they were treated as honored guests and every request they made was granted. Spending the next day in the common room, the Gracies regaled their fellow travelers with carefully edited tales of their journey and of Platonia.

Nevertheless, Huw felt the presence of the watchers and their eyes, making him uneasy. Huw quietly conveyed this to the other Graces, and they agreed in the finger speech to keep this information from their escort. Undoubtedly soldiers from Eldora would take orders from a Shadow.

The next day, the Gracies were prepared to journey the last two days to Platonia, when their Eldoran escort captain spoke with them early in the morning.

'I have received emergency orders from the Eldoran messenger corps during the night. A group of Brigands is rumored to lie east of here, marauding and pillaging, and my entire command must ride and stop them from causing more mayhem. You should remain here until we return, so that we can escort you home, but it might be a week or maybe longer until we can provide you escort.'

Thinking for a moment, Huw asked, 'Are there any reports of brigands blocking our way home?'

'No,' replied the captain, 'but I have no recent scouting reports from the north road. If there are any other Brigands they will be there.'

'Well, we will consider your proposal. Please go about your business, Captain.'

The captain called for the rest of his men to assemble, and in half an hour they left, cantering east of Barnhart and fanning out to find the Brigands.

As the dust from their horses settled, Berwyn turned to Huw. 'I cannot afford to be away from the inn any longer. Can't the Magi and the Vespre protect us?'

'Indeed they can, and much more important than your inn is the state of the Well of Life. We must recharge the waters so that the Bubblers can keep their magic and hopefully multiply and protect Platonia. If we take the grassy track, we should avoid any Brigands that might lie in ambush for us. Besides, this will give us an opportunity perhaps to capture one or both of the Shadows that are following us. Let us have our horses saddled so that we can depart.'

The Gracies rode along the stone road as it curved north and east well away from the Dark Forest until they found the grassy track freshly worn by the horses of the Kozaki, with deep puddles and mud everywhere after two days of heavy rain.

As the day wore on, the Gracies noted that the last of the buildings and farms of Men fell away. By the time evening fell, they were quite alone. Small streams of mist crept from the river and gently stole along the ground, forming temporary ghosts and mist creatures.

Camping for the night, Huw said, 'Toward the end of tomorrow we will pass through the Stadia, a raw limestone escarpment that forms a crude amphitheater on the east side of the road. If you shout from a certain point near its center, the sound will amplify and echo. I really annoyed my Elven escort when I first journeyed to Phoenicia by shouting much of the evening and even throwing rocks against the rock walls.'

'Sounds like you in your youth,' said Reggie. 'But we do not have time for a repeat performance tomorrow.'

'I know,' said Huw. 'So let's get some sleep and try to get home as fast as we can.'

As morning broke, the Gracies found themselves in country that was unkempt and wild; the only person they saw was a Man, who, seeing them on their horses, fled east and south. Soon, they came to the remnants of outbuildings and a few thatched huts, the remnants of the squatters' dwellings that had recently been vacated. Half-plowed fields, a small new graveyard, and piles of manure were the only other traces that there had been any Men here at all.

Riding the rest of the day, they saw small huts and a structure that had been burned. Two mounds had been dug near smaller graves that had spears of Kozak upon them; the fresh-cut turves distinguished the graves of riders from those they had slain in their forced relocation effort.

Shocked, Reggie said, 'I thought that the Riders were only going to encourage these people to relocate, not slay them and their families.'

'So did I,' Huw said sadly. 'While I am glad the squatters have left, it is both sad and disturbing that anyone was killed over these lands. Even worse that the riders would lie to us about how they persuaded these people to leave.'

'Perhaps they had no choice,' interjected Berwyn. 'Maybe they were attacked by the squatters.'

'What type of attack could simple farm folk mount against five hundred riders of Kozak?' retorted Reggie.

'We saw the attack the brigands mounted against the Bubblers and Greater Elves,' returned Berwyn, 'and even that arrogant Elf Lord Emedius nearly perished. We don't know what happened here.'

'Yes, we do,' said a solemn Rolly. 'Men fought and killed each other again, this time over farmland. What will be the next reason or prevarication? We know what they did to our ancestors, or why do we hide behind the Bubblers in Platonia? Men, no matter if they help us today, will always be our ultimate enemy.'

On that cheerful note, the Gracies continued north, hoping within the next few days to make Eastpointe, the ferry grounds of Platonia, and return to their homes. In camp that night, after the evening meal, they were enjoying some ale purchased at the last inn, when Huw strode to his baggage and extracted a small soft bundle that was all in black cloth. Returning to the fire, he opened it. It seemed to be a squat piece of round tree bark or perhaps a root, about three feet long, having a six foot black cord attached to it. The Gracies were completely perplexed.

'What is that?' asked Rolly.

'Wait and see,' said Huw with a smile. 'I don't even know if it will work. I only had one brief lesson.'

'What does it do?' asked Reggie.

'Hopefully it will help me call Eolus,' said Huw. All the Gracies knew that the Magi and the Vespre had not been seen since they left the riders of Kozak to return home.

'How?' asked Reggie. 'And why now, after dark? We can hardly expect to get anything done at this time of night.'

'To answer your first question, I am going to use this Woodwhistle. The Magi have a name for it that is nearly unpronounceable, so I will not even try and repeat it here,' said Huw. 'For the second, wait and see.'

Rising to his feet, he began spinning the Woodwhistle over his head until faint but deep sounds could be heard coming from it. Realizing he had to spin it faster, Huw let out all the cord, and the whistle suddenly made a moaning, crying sound similar to the sounds of the Magi. As he spun the whistle faster and slower, the pitch of the tone rose and fell and sometimes stopped all together. After spinning the whistle over his head for fifteen minutes or so, Huw carefully stopped the rotation of the whistle and, shaking the strain out of his arms, sat down.

'Well, that was a surprise, where did you get that?' asked Berwyn.

'From our ephemeral host,' replied Huw. 'Let us wait until Eolus comes to say more.'

Soon the Gracies heard a whispering murmur come from the south and east: the distant murmurings of the Vespre. Cloaking themselves in their own power, the Vespre were upon and around the Gracies before they actually noticed that they were close by.

Eolus strode, bearing the form of a Live Oak, stout but strong, into the circle a few minutes later, quietly greeting the Gracies. 'I see you remembered to use the Woodwhistle, though your song was terrible. It sounded like a rabbit in a snare.'

'Well, I only had a brief lesson from you, and all you said was to swing it over my head in a circle until it began to sing.'

'Yes, *sing* being the operative word, not *howl* and *shriek*,' snorted Eolus. 'But I am here regardless.'

'When and where did you get this whistle, much less learn how to use it?' asked Berwyn. 'We have been with you every minute of the way.'

'Not quite,' said Huw. 'The night after we left the Vale, after you fell asleep, I slipped away back toward the Vale and met Eolus there. He gave me the whistle and instructions as to how to use it in case we needed help before we arrived home.'

Berwyn again appeared at a loss for words.

Huw, meanwhile, turned to Eolus. 'You know of the Shadows following us?'

'Of course,' replied the Magi.

'Well, we are now going to catch them where they can't be helped by other Men.'

Bowing slightly, Eolus raised his hands to his mouth and let out a deep warbling cry. Many of the Vespre that surrounded them seemed to drift away, and all was quiet as the Gracies waited … for what, they could not say.

A few minutes later, the murmuring sigh of the Vespre reverberated in the near distance; a sudden high-pitched shriek and the sounds of a man in pain rapidly came toward them. The Gracies could see that it was another Shadow, clenched tightly between the moving branches of the Vespre; he had injured his arm badly while trying to escape.

Huw asked him his business and received the same stock phrases give to Priscus. Huw warned Eolus about the weapons of the Shadows, wanting to keep this one alive so that he could be questioned later by Priscus. Rasping out his frustration at being disarmed, the Shadow slumped quietly in his restraints, seeming to lose the will to fight. A sequence of murmurs and sighs came from all around the Gracies, rising and falling as if the wind were moving through summer branches at twilight, and Eolus responded in kind for a few moments and then was silent.

'Well, that was easier than I thought, but there is probably one more out there,' said Huw to Eolus.

'There is indeed,' said Eolus. 'The Vespre said he fled west toward the Dark Forest. He might have more fellows nearby, and the Vespre will keep an eye on him and see if there are any other rats running in the darkness. Now, for our captive, he should be tied up somewhere for the night.'

'Yes, but as soon as he is immobile, I am going to use my powers and see if I can get an answer once and for all as to what is they are doing following us.' As the Gracies rummaged in their packs for some rope, the injured Shadow said, 'Please, there is medicine in my belt pouch, I can use it to tend my wound.'

Looking coldly at him, Huw rummaged in the Shadow's pouch, finding a small jar of salve. This he applied to the man's wound, after which the Shadow asked for the small phial in his pouch, as it contained an extract for pain. Seeing that the man's shoulder was possibly dislocated or broken, Huw extracted a small, very thick glass phial, firmly stoppered, from the man's pouch.

'Place it in my mouth and I will remove the cork,' said the Shadow. 'I will then be much more at ease.'

'Wait,' said Huw. 'Let us examine it first to make sure that he stays alive. The clear liquid phial proved difficult to uncork, until Reggie used a very small pen knife. The Gracies passed it around, smelling it.

Rolly said after sniffing and tasting it, 'It smells and tastes like willow bark tea, with perhaps a little oil of southern spice. It should do little one way or another, so he can have it.'

The Vespre shifted their position, tilting the man forward so Huw could give him his medicine. Clenching the bottle in his teeth, the Shadow suddenly bit down on the glass and sucked the liquid into his mouth, his lips red with the blood of the cuts of the glass. Trying to remove the broken glass carefully, Huw saw the Shadow's eyes roll back into his head, his body spasming and twitching, a soft hiss escaping from clenched lips, and then the body was limp as a rag doll.

Stamping his feet in rage and frustration, Huw said, 'He is dead! The phial contained a poison somehow, not willow bark tea.' Holding the remains of the phial close to the fire, Huw observed that the phial was actually two glass containers, with one inside the other. The inner chamber was accessible by the end with the stopper, while the other chamber, presumably filled with poison, had been sealed with glass or some other substance. Regardless, the double-walled phial was undetectable until it was used. Shaking his head at the complexity of the tools employed by the Shadows, especially those used to take their own lives, Huw said little.

'He is certainly at ease now, however,' said Berwyn sardonically.

Muttering darkly that they must be more careful in the future if they were ever going to learn why the Shadows were following them, and what they hoped to accomplish, Huw was displeased with his lack of vigilance. The Vespre stripped the Shadow out of his clothing and took the body away for burial, and a search of the clothes turned up nothing.

'Maybe his companion will be caught alive and we can keep him that way,' said Huw. 'Let us now try and get some rest.'

Turning in, the Gracies slept more soundly than they had so far on their homeward journey, knowing the Vespre and Eolus would keep watch through the night.

The next day, the road began skirting the eastern edge of the Dark Forest. The Gracies recalled their boat trip with mild trepidation, hoping that they would never be asked to venture in there again.

They were nearing the outcropping of limestone, and Huw cheerfully mentioned the Stadia again and retold the same stories until Berwyn grumped that fairly soon he could tell the stories himself.

As they entered the edge of the Stadia, a terrible sound echoed and reverberated from their right, but from the edge of the forest there was only silence. Again the sound came, and the scrub trees that filled the Stadia began to move; from the edge of the foliage emerged terrible forms, tall and hideous. Pale faces with jet black hair and expressions twisted in a frenzied omnipresent hatred could not disguise the Elvish features underneath. Their dark eyes were manic, and flecks of foam came from their mouths. Bright blue streaks lay upon their faces, and their bodies were naked except for a crude loincloth. Their arms ended in terrible hands twisted and bent, their long fingers ending in broken claws.

Huw reached out with his enhanced senses and found only a terrible feeling of determination to destroy all life and a hint of a terrible purpose behind them. Huw recognized them as Dark Elves, twisted and united in purpose more powerful than Dark Elves before them. Huw summoned up his powers; pink streamers left his extended hands but were absorbed by the Dark Elves without any obvious effect. Cupping their hands to their mouths, they let loose the terrible sound again, determined to drive their prey before them in a terrible panic. Already, the Gracies could barely control their mounts, and Berwyn demanded, 'Do something, Huw!'

'I will!' he replied. Taking a mental and physical breath, he gathered his powers and used them against the closest Dark Elf. This time, the pink fires were not absorbed. Instead, they began running up and down the body of the Dark Elf, the magic of life and hope battling with the magic of death and despair. The battle was brief, consuming less than a minute, and the Gracies were encouraged when the Dark Elf gave a discordant shriek and slumped to the ground.

Yet instead of scattering, as legend would have it, the Dark Elves showed a singular purpose when they bent and picked up great cudgels made from tree branches, sinews of deer, and sharp rocks. They then charged toward the Gracies. Huw knew that they were done for, until, with a hissing as of foam upon the sea, the Vespre charged in from their escort points, led by Eolus, and formed a shield of magical life around the Gracies.

'Gather yourself again!' shouted Eolus. 'Attack the nearest Dark Elf! We will hold them until you can kill them all.'

Huw faltered for a moment; his powers were for life, not death.

'You can't hesitate,' cried Berwyn. 'Try and find a peaceful solution and we will be dead. Strike now!'

Striking again, Huw saw another Dark Elf fall. But they continued to lope toward the Gracies. Momentarily they dropped their clubs, and, placing their hands against their mouths, they let forth their terrible cry again. Beginning on a frequency beyond the hearing of the Gracies, but not of the Vespre, the sound grew in power as it raced down through the sound spectrum to a frequency felt rather than heard. With that, five of the closest Vespre burst into flame, their cries terrible as they were consumed by the dark sound of the Dark Elves.

Shocked, even Huw did not prepare another assault as more Vespre fell to the sonic barrage. Seeing more than twenty of the Dark Elves, Berwyn's book-keeping mind worked quickly. Ignoring Huw, who was too shocked to be of help right now, he charged the few yards to Eolus and screamed, 'You must do something!'

'I am trying,' said Eolus. 'I have never seen or felt anything like this before.'

Raising their clubs, the Dark Elves advanced another ten yards, then dropped them again as another sonic barrage consumed more of the Vespre. Desperately, Eolus summoned the powers of life within him. Coordinating with Huw, who had been jolted out of his horror by a determined Berwyn riding back to him and slapping him across the face, the Magi sent a pink glow over the Vespre and their charges, deflecting the next attack. But the Dark Elves grabbed their clubs and moved forward until they were only fifty feet away. There they paused and unleashed several more sonic barrages. The pink glow sheltered the Vespre, but one of their remaining twenty-two decided to attack the Dark Elves directly. As he neared his intended target, a shortened version of the terrible cry went up, weaker than the usual assault, but enough to turn the Vespre into a pyre, his life going up in a terrible smoke. The sonic barrage continued, taking its toll on

Eolus and Huw, until finally Huw slumped against his horse. Seeing their defeat at hand, Eolus and the Vespre spent the last of their magic to momentarily hold the Dark Elves at bay.

'There is only one path not blocked,' said Eolus. 'We must retreat into the Dark Forest.'

'You can't be serious,' said Berwyn. 'You know that no one who entered the forest ever survived to tell the tale, except for that one expedition of Men, and they lost three-fourths of their party by the second day and were driven out by the Demons of the Wood.'

'I am aware of the history of the Dark Forest, thank you,' said Eolus. 'But the outcome will be different now, for not only am I here, but the remaining Vespre should be able to help stem the powers of the Demons of the Wood.'

'Your powers have been useless today!' screamed Berwyn. 'Most of your friends are dead. Your powers will be even less useful against the Wood Demons. Let us charge through the northern edge—perhaps some of us will make it home.'

'That's where their reinforcements are waiting quietly for us,' said Eolus. 'I can feel them even now. The way north is a trap. Only the forest can offer us some refuge.'

'How?' demanded Berwyn.

But with that last question the magical protection failed, and the Dark Elves charged, this time intent upon killing the Gracies and destroying their precious cargo. Berwyn's question went unanswered.

The Gracies galloped into the forest as Eolus summoned the Vespre to retreat to the forest edge as well. Only twelve Vespre made it into the forest, but, drawing upon the strong forces of life that ran through the forest, Huw and Eolus were able to form a stronger magical protection against the Dark Elves. Several Dark Elves tried to penetrate into the forest but were consumed by the protection created by a revived Huw and Eolus. The sonic barrage failed as it was no longer reflected and focused by the unique features of the Stadia, absorbed instead by the lush undergrowth. Stalemate ensued as the Dark Elves realized that their quarry was out of reach. They extended their lines north and south of the point of entry, determined to let the forest do their work for them.

Pausing and gasping in his saddle, Huw said, 'Wait, I must catch my breath, and then we must go deeper into the forest.'

'Deeper, are you mad?' said Berwyn. 'These creatures are bad enough, but if we ride close to the forest edge, we can get behind them and escape to the fords.'

'No,' said Huw, 'that is what they expect. Besides, how do you intend to ride through the forest close enough to the edge to escape without the Dark Elves seeing us? Look at the density of the trees and the undergrowth. Except for an occasional deer path or trail created by the Wood Demons who are reputed to live here, we would be forced to crawl through the forest, with our supplies limited. No, our only choice is to go forward. See, even now there is a path wide enough for our horses to trot.'

Not knowing what to say, Berwyn and the Gracies turned their attention to riding north and west, hoping to emerge on the southern edge of Platonia and then swimming the river to safety, if necessary with the help of the Bubblers.

Eolus was now walking beside them, forcing their path wider through the trees and the underbrush, ignoring the whispers of the trees, their branches and leaves talking in the wind. The news ran before them: Magi had come after millennia in isolation. Eolus knew the speech of most trees, but these eluded him; the language had changed, isolated too long. Still, the general content could be gleaned as the branches of ancient trees moved in a nonexistent zephyr, conveying the amazing news.

From far away there was a dark echo, a ripple of discontent that grew louder as they found the banks of the Beadle. The Wood Demons knew of them, and they were not pleased with another power entering their realm. Mortals were one thing; they could be dealt with easily. But here was competition for the heart of their forest and a genuine threat to their power. They would not take this challenge lightly.

Soon the branches were moving in waves from north to south and back again. The path the Gracies were following suddenly ended in small meres and swamps, forcing them to backtrack and find new pathways forward. Submerged roots caused their horses to stumble, and the Gracies had many an unkind branch slap them in their faces. Vines fell from trees and tangled their limbs and their hair, tugging at the straps of their baggage horses, causing them to whinny and snort in frustration. Reggie and Rolly were entangled in vines that reached around their throats and mysteriously pulled backwards up into the trees. Eolus was momentarily beset by branches, and it was several frantic seconds before Huw and Berwyn were able to cut the vines from Reggie and Rolly. Gasping for breath, the Gracies could not proceed for several moments.

Eolus was forced against his love for trees to snap a small ash tree in half that had thoroughly tangled his limbs before the party slowly became ordered on the pathway again.

Worse, now bright blue flowers and twisted vines came from the surrounding foliage and encircled them, moving rapidly forward in snakelike motions and touching the Gracies with their beautiful petals. Bright red weals rose from their contact. Reggie and Rolly and Berwyn went into convulsions as the poisons from the terrible Doll's Eye flowers spread rapidly through their bodies, shutting down their hearts and lungs. Eolus was beset and unable to come to their aid, and even the Vespre in the distance were stymied by this brutal attack.

Huw knew he had to act quickly. Stretching out his hands, he called the magic of the Gemwings and of the Vale to his mind. A great golden glow spread about him, infused with pink. The golden glow struck out at the Doll's Eyes, dropping the deadly flowers from their stalks and leaving nothing but writhing headless green ropes flailing without purpose. Huw then extended his arms to his fallen companions, and the pink glow enveloped them within its healing touch. Feeling that the vines were creations of the Wood Demons, Huw had no reservations in destroying them.

The poison was quite complex, and Huw spent several minutes adjusting this spell of healing until he had the correct sequence and could begin destroying the poison within his friends. Soon they were able to sit up, the bright weals of death fading quickly upon their skin. Gathering a shuddering breath, they were about to shout at Huw and demand that they leave this green animated hell and take their chances with the Dark Elves, when they noted that Huw was still in his trance. A sudden glow emanated from Huw, flashing pink and gold, and the Gracies felt the magic cover their bodies, a protective shield against the magical attacks of the Wood Demons.

This did not prevent the ordinary assault of the forest from continuing, however, and the Gracies were besieged again. Not only plants and trees, but now the animals and insects of the Dark Forest came to challenge them. Hornets and bees flew and stung as the Gracies yelped and swatted. Midges came as dark clouds, biting and stinging as they filled the Gracies' eyes, noses and mouths with hundreds of winged bodies. A large turtle lurched out of the stream and bit Reggie on the foot, causing him to fall into the river. Rescued by Eolus, he sat cursing and bleeding on the remnants of the trail. Birds now came, reaching for their eyes and clawing at their faces. A skunk came and was about to unleash its foul essence when it was picked up by Eolus and hurled gently but firmly into the river. Finally, several beavers emerged from the river and began gnawing at Eolus's feet, cracking their teeth against his impenetrable skin. Struggling to free themselves from their assailants, the Gracies were about to finally give up hope and leave the Forest as quickly as they had arrived, when the assault upon them suddenly lessened.

Moving forward again, they proceeded north along the river, as the tension of the forest rose rapidly, though they were not the targets this time; it was Eolus and the Vespre who continued to upset the balance. The very earth opened at Eolus's feet. Roots grew out of the ground, ensnaring his feet, trying to topple him onto the forest floor. Stones moved and created sparks, setting piles of dry twigs and leaves aflame, scorching at the toes of the Magi. The wind rose in fierce gusts, blowing and hissing through the woods. A violent circular cloud appeared, gray and dark; rain spat from its center and lightning flickered around its edges. Vast and dark, it lowered itself from a sky clear just minutes ago, uprooting trees and shrubs and dragging Berwyn above the ground and into the sky. Eolus was able to snatch Berwyn's foot from the air and hold him as his other arm encompassed the Gracies in safety. Huw looked down to avoid the raging wind and saw that Eolus's feet had become stone, plunging deep into the soil to anchor his body and those of the Gracies, holding fast as the wind moaned and screamed around them.

Grumbling aloud, Eolus paused, raising his arms and singing a deep song, notes so low they were beneath hearing and the Gracies only felt them in their chests, resonating powerfully within their very bones. Long did this song go on as the Gracies were assaulted anew and more fiercely than before. Perceiving that the Forest could not successfully attack Eolus, it meant to drive the Gracies out and have the Magi follow.

'Close your eyes and mouth,' said Huw. 'Stand fast, for this assault cannot last.' Suddenly the waves in the trees became more erratic, less rhythmic, and Eolus stopped his song and chuckled aloud.

'Powerful are these Wood Demons who have stood in the forest for seasons uncounted, but not powerful enough. I have enjoyed dueling with them from afar, but you were nearly lost, and this is not something that I could have allowed. Now the ring is closed and their magic is confined.'

With that, Eolus stopped in his tracks and laughed a great laugh. The trees above them seemed to shudder and shake, as if casting off a spell from afar.

A soft southern breath of air tugged at the Gracies' hair, and above them the trees began to move individually, no longer in synchronous undulations that had conveyed the Demons' thoughts and will throughout the forest.

Pausing to tend their stings and bites, scratches and welts, the Gracies were less than enthused about continuing their journey, but they had to press on or sleep here.

Soon, as dusk was upon them, they emerged into a clearing where sat the great circle of trees that defined the heart of the Wood Demons.

In actuality, as Eolus explained to the Gracies, these were no demons but lesser Magi who had fled the Vale long ago, driven forth by Priscus and the other Magi. These lesser Magi had embraced evil, wanting to spread beyond the Vale and choke the world with plants and trees, bringing Nostraterra beneath their sway. The immorality of their desires was thwarted by the impracticality of planting foliage that would take centuries before it could pull magic the earth. Priscus and the others had tried to guide the rebellious Magi back to the light and away from the darkness, but instead had provoked an open conflict in which the lesser Magi were defeated and fled into the darkest forest they could find. Swiftly filling the forest with their twisted vision, they placed themselves in the heart of the Dark Forest. Now, weakened by their conflict with Priscus and his allies, they were forced to give up their transient forms and take root, literally, in the tallest of the trees of this forest.

Knowing they were terribly vulnerable to an assault by immortals and mortals alike, bearing axes or fire, they extended their powers into the rest of the forest, forcing all life and all forces of nature to stand with them and obey their ultimate command: kill all who enter here.

Prior to this journey, Priscus and the rest of the Magi had hoped they could alter the balance within this forest and bring an enforced peace to this land. The lesser Magi had preserved this forest against encroachment, something the Magi respected and wanted continued. Eolus told the Gracies that he and the Vespre were going to try and regulate the powers of the Dark Magi. While they would no longer allow their former brethren to kill indiscriminately, they would allow them to protect their forest with deadly force if needed. Besides, for now, they needed their help against the Dark Elves, creating a hidden path free from observance or attack by the Dark Elves.

As the Gracies listened to this tale, they saw that the great circle of the Dark Magi was itself encircled by strategically placed shadowy shapes. The great dark shapes of the Vespre with their ocular confounding mist were slowly but inexorably circling the Dark Magi, beating back their mighty voices with their chorus. The Gracies watched this spectacle, sensing something of the contest raging in front of them. The Dark Magi were sending all of their thoughts out to the rest of the forest, only to have their will reflected back into the circle by the Vespre.

Feelings of helpless anger would occasionally emerge from gaps in the Vespre circle. Here and there, an individual tree would take instructions from the Wood Demons; the shifting gap allowed only a general susurration in the closest trees. Above the circle of the Vespre, the Wood Demons' magical emanations were reflected back upon them; the very air seemed to roil and dance with energy. A small branch from a spreading Elm tree that crossed the circle above the Vespre began to smolder as the Demons put forth the last of their strength in their desire to break through the power of the Vespre. One final surge of power filled the circle; the air filled with red lights and sparks, kindling some of the nearby branches, but it broke upon the indomitable will of the Vespre, scattering and reflecting back into the circle, setting the enclosed brush alight. Several rabbits and squirrels leapt from the burning circle, and singed birds perched in the branches of the Vespre. The last emergent magic of the Demons had consumed anything that had remained within the circle, their impotent rage funneled into the very forest they loved.

The power rapidly subsided; the entire forest seemed to understand that the contest was over. The Demons were defeated for now, and creatures that had legs or wings instead of roots could freely move through the forest.

Sighing at the number of lives that had been lost during the dominion of the Demons, Eolus said, 'We should have come here sooner to take charge of this forest, but we lacked the blending of your mortal abilities, Huw; only with your help did we win the argument today. The legends of the strength of the Wood Demons were not exaggerated. It is sad for us that I did not believe you and prepare better for the possibility that we might be forced into these woods somehow. If they consent to our will; they could aid us much in protecting this forest from those who would harm it and allow those who would help the forest to pass through without assault. Alas, even the hearts of trees can go black with time.'

'Indeed,' said Huw. 'But now we must camp for the night and rest, for I am exhausted and will not be able to lend you any more aid without refreshment. Hopefully you and the Vespre can handle the demons without me for tonight.'

'We can,' said Eolus, 'but let us travel a bit farther. There is a clearing that the Vespre detected with a spring that will be a bit more comfortable for you.'

As the Gracies wondered how they were supposed to see, a figure appeared before them; an old man clothed in brown. A dark brown hat was on his head, a gnarled staff of dark wood clutched in his hand. The staff looked ancient, and, to Reggie's trained eye, it was of holly, deep and rich with grain and the endless marks of time. Gray was the old man's hair, with streaks of brown running through it, and brown were his eyes under shaggy brows. Various stains were upon his robes, and his cloak looked as travel worn as he did.

'Well, now, this is a sight,' said the figure. 'Gracies, Magi and Vespre all together in my forest; there must be a great tale behind this.'

Huw was so exhausted that he thought the figure a vision until he drew closer to it. 'I do not know your name, but we need your aid.'

'That you shall have and perhaps more,' replied the figure. 'Let us go to my home.'

'How can we see?' asked Berwyn. 'Night is upon us.'

With that, the figure gestured slightly, and clouds of fireflies gathered around their mounts, providing faint but golden illumination; enough for their horses to see the track. The Gracies slowly moved along the path, hearing the nightly noises of the forest. The brooding darkness of the will of the forest was spent, leaving a peaceful echo amongst the trees. Night birds and small creatures moved in the undergrowth and branches above them, with malice toward none. The moon shone down in gaps in the canopy, silver hues glancing off the dark soft waters of streams running down to the Beadle. They felt sleep wash over them as the fatigue from their journey and today's battle began to mount.

Soon they saw a golden light coming from an open doorway; a house built of stone, covered in moss and shaded by maple trees stood there, with a stone stable standing nearby. A spring bubbled out of the ground at their feet. Filling a stone-lined pool, it burbled happily as it ran down to the river.

Walking to the open doorway, Eolus glanced at the door, which was far too short to fit his tall form, and said, 'For the first time since you left the Vale, I truly think that you Gracies are in no danger.' Bidding them goodnight, he went off in search of a cool place to refresh the tree shape that he had taken upon their entrance into the forest.

The Gracies went into the main room and saw that the dark figure who had met them in the forest was sitting at a table, sipping a glass mug of beer. Four other glass mugs were on the table, frosted with ice, alongside a tall pitcher of rich brown ale, barely visible through the thick frost upon it.

Berwyn wondered how the mugs and pitcher had come to be covered in ice; it was early summer, and while the evening was cool, there certainly was no snow around. Too tired to ask questions, he gratefully extended his hand and poured beer for his friends.

A deep voice spoke out, and Berwyn saw the flash of the man's eyes. 'Aye, my little friends! You are welcome here. Come and enjoy a glass of beer with me.'

Looking at the Gracies, the old Man said, 'Huw, son of Heflin; Berwyn, son of Largo; Reginard, son of Ifan; Rolant, son of Marmaduke, well met, well met indeed. I had hoped that I would meet you soon, but now you have come in such ancient and august company that no one could have foreseen it.' Chuckling, he turned to his beer again.

'Forgive me, Father, who are you?' asked Berwyn. 'Clearly you know us, but do we know you?'

Smiling, the man asked, 'Can none of you name my name? Even you, my little lore-master, you do not know me?'

'I think I do,' said Huw. 'But I thought you were gone out of tales long ago.'

'Indeed, I am that person. Name me now so your friends will believe the truth,' said the old man.

'He is Demetrius, the last of the Earth Spirits in Nostraterra,' said Huw.

'The last,' snorted Demetrius. 'No, I don't think so, I am afraid. But I am indeed Demetrius.'

'What do you mean that you are not the last?' asked Huw.

'Never mind, that is a tale for tomorrow,' said Demetrius. 'Now finish your mugs of beer. Then you must wash, and, after, I will tend your wounds. Then we can have our supper and get some rest. The tales will keep until then.'

'Will you tell of yourself then, Master?' asked Huw, draining his mug. 'Truly I thought the last of the Earth Spirits were departed from Nostraterra.'

'I will tell you some of it in the morning, but some things must be told over time, if at all,' said Demetrius. 'Now go and tend to yourselves.'

The Gracies went down the hall at Demetrius' direction, the flagstones cool beneath their feet. They came to a bathing room, where a cauldron of water was at a steady boil and four fresh wooden tubs had been set out for them. Berwyn was amazed again, as the cauldron boiled without any visible flames or heat and the tubs were ready as if long prepared. Four thick soft cloth robes were hanging on hooks, with matching warm wool slippers and thick towels. When he spoke these thoughts aloud, Huw replied, 'Indeed, we seem to have been anticipated. Let us wash quickly and return to our host.'

Entering the main room again, the robed Gracies stood still as Demetrius gently ran his hands up and down their bodies, murmuring gently under his breath. He used his staff to touch the deep cut on Reggie's foot, and the Gracies watched enthralled as it swiftly grew closed. Then, as Demetrius did the same to the rest of them, they felt the stings and cuts disappear from their hands and faces.

Gesturing at the Gracies to sit, Demetrius said, 'Now let us eat well and rest the night, for the morning will bring new counsel.'

The Gracies sat down to the table; they were served only fruits, cheeses, and breads: no meat was served at the table of Demetrius. More rich ale, dark and sweet, complex and fruity, the strongest the Gracies had ever tasted, however, did much to alleviate their fear and fatigue, flowing to their hearts like wine. Soon they were singing and laughing, shrugging off the stains of their travels. When they finally pushed back their chairs, sated, Demetrius pulled out a pipe and, after lighting it, began to suck on it lustily until he had a fine plume of fragrant herb smoke rising around his head.

'Now, my young Gracies, tell me your tale, and you shall hear mine on the morrow,' said Demetrius. 'Which of you will begin?'

Reggie begged to tell the tale, as he had first seen the Gemwings on the Plateau. Demetrius seemed to doze through their tale, and only opened his eyes when the Gracies told of their journey to the Vale and to Eldora.

Finishing their recitation, Huw said, 'Well, now you have heard our tale. Will you tell us yours?'

'It is late, near midnight; you Gracies are very tired after your battles today. You are safe in my house from the Dark Elves. Rest easy and we will speak in the morning.'

He led the Gracies to rooms down the hall, where they were quickly ensconced within soft cotton sheets and white wool blankets. The moon was riding low in the western sky, and the Gracies drifted off to sleep with small moonbeams coming through their window, winking through the trees.

The next morning, they arose and had a good breakfast, with eggs hot from the pan, toasted bread, fruit jams and fresh tomatoes, taking advantage of Demetrius' pantry. Demetrius came into the house then, with a large black raven perched on his shoulder with a gray head going bald, and, giving it a piece of fried egg from the pan off the stove, Demetrius began speaking to it in a tongue that even Huw did not recognize, much less understand. The attention of the Gracies was suddenly drawn to his brown robes, alive with motion. A squirrel poked its head out and chattered at them until Demetrius soothed it with his hands and made small, high-pitched noises that the Gracies could only guess were words that the squirrel could understand. Within a few more minutes, a weasel, a small round bird that looked like a quail, several mice, a toad, and others had made their appearance. Sitting down in their chairs, the Gracies were surprised by a loud flapping sound as a brightly colored bird flew into the room; what it was, and where it came from, they had no idea. It suddenly began speaking in a human voice that mimicked Demetrius' perfectly, and for a moment they were uncertain as to whether he or the bird was speaking.

Eolus, now present with his leafy shadow darkening the open doorway, spoke. 'If your menagerie is done talking and showing off, perhaps we could have your tale and then determine what is to be done with the Wood Demons and how we can escape the Dark Elves.'

Demetrius chuckled and said, 'My menagerie, as you call them, are quite finished with their morning conversation, and they will not speak unless I ask them questions. It was high time the Wood Demons were reminded there were other ancient powers in this world, and that they must exercise some restraint if they want to be treated respectfully.'

'Restraint,' said Eolus. 'That is the last thing that they know. Their hearts are black, wanting to rule this forest without restriction. You cannot imagine the problem we Magi had with them in the Vale before their exile. But you have said nothing about the Dark Elves.'

'I will travel with the Gracies and you and your Vespre, seeing all of you safely into Platonia. You need not fear the Dark Elves.'

'Very well,' said a relieved Eolus. 'Now tell the Gracies your tale so that they understand who you are and why you are here.'

Chuckling, Demetrius, said, 'Yes, it is time for my tale. You Gracies should get comfortable on the couches in the sitting room.'

Great was his tale and many hours did it consume, and it was known to none but Demetrius. In the beginning he offered a brief synopsis so that they would not lose the thread of his story.

'Long ago, I arose in Nostraterra, approximately two thousand years ago. I was the first Earth Spirit that was summoned by the Men who now comprise the kingdom of Eldora, through their first crude magic. I taught Men farming and animal husbandry, to love the land and the forests. I taught them the necessity of balance. But Men were not satisfied with simply existing. They wanted more knowledge than I could provide, to build with metal and stone and to learn alchemy, so that in their eyes they could "progress" as a people. They used their expanded knowledge to summon two other Earth Spirits, one who taught them metallurgy and stone work, the other alchemy. The Earth Spirit who taught them metal and stone soon tired of teaching and wanted to lead the race of Men along his own path. Rejected by Men, this Earth Spirit left peaceably, telling me he would go forth into the east and south in search of Men who would follow him.

'The other Earth Spirit was greedily welcomed by Men, as he taught them Alchemy, with all of the terrible knowledge that comes with such study. As his influence grew, Men became very powerful, full of the secrets of the earth. Their Alchemy equaled the magic of the Elves and the Dwarves, and it set the balance of Nostraterra onto an uneasy tripod of power. Then Men became proud and disdainful of the earth, slaying beasts without reason, cutting down the forests for personal enrichment, no longer wishing to live in harmony with the earth and the creatures and plants that were here before them. Much debate did I have with the ancient alchemists and the kings of Men, but to no avail, so at last I withdrew my aid and left their realms, wandering the great lands in search of a reason and purpose to my existence.

'Men were betrayed by their own lust for power as the Alchemical Earth Spirit's influence grew, controlling the majority of Alchemists, threatening to take over Eldora. The King of Eldora discovered the danger, demanding that the Earth Spirit cease his activities. The Earth Spirit refused, and seeing the entire army of Eldora assembled to assail him, he fled, taking some of his followers with him. Neither Earth Spirit has been heard from again; they have never returned. What has come of them, I do not know, but I fear the worst.'

'But what of you?' asked Huw. 'What part did you play in the defeat of Magnar, and why are you still here?'

'I was the one who taught your forefathers the true nature of the magic contained in the Waters of Life in the infinite well in the center of Platonia. For centuries they had stumbled along the edge of this particular puzzle, making minor use of the true powers of the waters. By blending the life of a Gracie willingly given, with the waters, they could make a weapon of life and love that would destroy any weapon of hate. Of course, I gave Emedius a nudge that the magic of your people was critical to the success of the forces arrayed against Magnar, and thankfully he listened to me; a terrible force of darkness was banished forever. I cared little for Men and Dwarves, though I hoped that the Elves would prevail; my love was for the earth itself and the forests that harbor life in all its forms.

'Sadly there is little left of the ancient forests, just pockets here and there. The Dark Forest, as you Gracies know it, only survived because the Wood Demons stopped Men from felling these trees. Long were Men distracted from destroying the forests during the Great War, but that ended with the fall of Magnar, and now Men are gathering, attacking the trees so their farms and forges can expand yet again. Today, however, the ancient magic is nearly gone, and there is little to stop the power of Men and their desire to conquer the entire world. I remain because I wish to save the forests and all that live within them. I did not know what else to do when Magnar fell. There is no one to help the animals and the trees but me. The Magi were far away, locked within their small land, and there was little that could be done to bring them forth. Until, that is, you were fortunate enough to find the Gemwings, my good Gracies. That alone could entice the Magi and the Vespre to leave their glorious glades.

'Now we have the chance, now we have the choice, to preserve what is left and to restore a balance to Nostraterra. There are places that have never known the thud of an axe or the high buzz of an arrow. There are still creatures who walk the earth, unsullied by the hand of Man, Dwarf or Elf, but they are few in number. With your help and the help of the Magi, perhaps they can be saved from the axe and the trap. Even my power is limited, however. I cannot change the face of Nostraterra alone. I cannot be everywhere at once. You must go forth from your land and make contact with Elves and those Men and Dwarves who are of good heart, willing to protect the forests. You must find those trees and animals most in need of protection, so there is at least some vestige of the green and quiet beauty that once filled this land from the mountains to the sea. When you have found those last wild islands of trees and beasts, I can come and perhaps so can the Magi. Now I have told you my tale. Ask what questions you like, and I will answer them if I can.'

Rising before Huw could say anything, Berwyn burst out, 'This is well and good that you want to preserve the forests and the beasts, but it is not a job for me! It is high time I returned to my inn. I have a business to run, and I do not have time to go on endless marches through forgotten forests, no matter how noble the reason.'

'Sit down, Berwyn,' said Huw firmly. 'This is not a request that we can lightly turn down. Why us, Demetrius? Why can't you go yourself? Surely you and your animal friends could see the needs of the forest and the creatures better than we can.'

'Certainly my friends can aid us in covering vast distances quickly, but they can only tell me what they see from the inside, not the outside. They would not be able to tell me about the Men or others who were arrayed against them, only that they were suffering. Even hawks and aeagles could only give me the number and type of each mortal who was attacking the forests; they cannot communicate to those that are there that they need to leave the forests alone. As for me, my power has always been one of knowledge, of healing and communication; I can only compel others with great effort. I teach and encourage, persuade and preserve, not conquer. Only when there is a direct and immediate threat to me or my friends can I contest and stop the will of another. Therefore, I can only stop what I currently see and experience. I cannot be everywhere at once, so I can either traipse around Nostraterra in vain, or choose one small place, as the Wood Demons and Magi have, as a refuge. I want to do more than that. If you help me, I can identify the places at greatest risk and seek to persuade those who would harm the forests and the creatures to leave them alone, or I can direct those allies that I may make with your help to act on the forests' behalf.'

Pondering this, Huw said, 'It seems we have a difficult choice. Are there no others upon whom you could call?'

'Whom should I ask?' said Demetrius. 'Most Men and some Dwarves are the source of this problem, not the solution. The Greater Elves are too few; they must defend their own lands from the encroachment of mortals. The Lesser Elves are responsible for their forest realms. They have numbers, but they have their own responsibilities. No, it must be you Gracies, for you know what it is like to have your own land threatened, your way of life taken from you. You know how hard it is to protect that which you love and the sacrifices involved. Even now your land is under siege. You depend upon the good will of the kings of Eldora and Kozak to procure your safety. But how long will Platonia be safe? A year? A hundred years? What happens when the current kings die? Will the next kings share the current kings' sense of obligation and nobility? You must act to save your own land, to save what you hold so dear to you. Since you must actively protect your homes, it is in your best interests to protect the trees and the animals as well.'

At that moment, a young fawn entered the room on wobbly legs, its deep brown eyes dewy with newborn tears. Innocence and wonder emanated from this most fragile and harmless of creatures. No stain lay upon its soul, and Demetrius extended his powers, allowing the Gracies to feel what the first days of their own lives must have felt like. The Gracies stared open-mouthed; never had a forest creature come into their midst as this most fragile of creatures now did. Softy it approached them, thrusting its nose toward the smell of milk on the table. Gently it nuzzled the hand of Demetrius and then turned toward the Gracies, its innocent eyes looking up to them with trust and love. The Gracies were entranced by this joy in newfound life, which filled them with peace and joy.

Slowly, the fawn walked toward Berwyn and laid her soft head in his lap. Unbidden, his hand came up from the armrest of the chair, and he began to stroke her head and neck lovingly. There were no sounds now, no speeches or words from anyone, only the feeling that innocent life was breathing its first breath and taking its first steps into a very wide world. The Gracies were captivated by the fawn, each of them remembering how they had felt long ago. The earliest memories of childhood, when no one was wiser than your father, no one more caring than your mother when she kissed your first skinned knee.

The Gracies rose and some knelt, others stood, each of them stroking the beautiful delicate creature. The Gracies saw the world for a moment through her eyes, the bright colors and rich smells of the world around her. She had been born in a deep copse of bracken in the forest, her first sights and sounds those of her mother breathing heavily with the exertions of her birth.

'Quickly now,' her mother had gasped in the speech of the deer, 'you must rise to your feet, you must be able to run. The two-legs will always chase you and will kill you if they can.'

Falling a few times and finally rising to her chest, the fawn had finally stood after an hour of hard labor on her own tiny legs. Turning to nurse, she drank deeply until her small belly was full. Her mother then climbed to her own weary legs and slowly moved from the sheltering bracken into the forest proper. Pausing to eat the tender grasses at the edge of the clearing, her mother was filled with joy at her daughter's birth, but was fearful of what the world held for her. Suddenly she and her daughter heard a summons to come to the old house in the forest and meet with the father of the beasts. That is how she and the other creatures knew Demetrius, the father and protector of all of them.

Now the fawn had been asked to meet with the father and his friends, and the Gracies were deeply moved by her presence. Slowly they removed their hands, knowing instinctively that they were to return within themselves, enriched by their experience, but they must exist within the confines of their mortal shells.

Suddenly a high-pitched scream came from outside the house, and Demetrius was on his feet immediately, running through the door. The Gracies were directly behind him, but the fawn outran them all. Straight to a small set of bushes she ran, bleating for her mother. Demetrius stopped at the edge of the bushes and knelt over something that the Gracies could not initially see. Berwyn was the first to move through the bushes and see the mother of the fawn lying there in a pool of her own blood, choking and gasping for air. An arrow protruded from her side, just behind her front leg.

The Gracies all were gathered now. 'Can't we do something for her?' asked Berwyn. 'We can't just let her die.'

'There is nothing to be done,' said Demetrius. 'Her life has been stolen from her. All we can do is ease the pain of her going.' Demetrius laid his hands on her head, whispering to her to be still, that she was going to be free from the confines of her life and free from its pain.

Huw refused to accept Demetrius' pronouncement. He extended his arms, and the great pink glow flowed from his fingertips, enveloping the doe as she lay dying. Huw entwined his spirit with that of the dying deer, and he bade her hold on as the other Gracies drew forth the arrow and tried to staunch the flow of her hot blood onto the forest floor. But even Huw's powers from the Vale were insufficient. Raging at his futility, he knew that all he was accomplishing was prolonging her pain. Her fate had been decided the moment this hateful arrow had left its string. Feeling more helpless and hopeless than at any time of his life, he withdrew his powers, and his attempts to save her life ended. He sat defeated upon the ground, tears streaming down his face.

The rest of the Gracies gathered around and extended their hands to her sides. As they touched her, they could see again through the eyes of another. The horrible agony of the arrow wound in her flesh, every labored breath a torment, the colors slowly fading from the world around her.

'*The two legs,*' thought the doe. '*The two legs have hurt me when Father said they would not. Why did he tell me that we would be safe with the two legs?*'

The pain grew from her side and spread throughout her body, her heart accelerating in a futile race against death. Her last desperate thoughts echoed in her mind, her spirit in torment and fear. 'My daughter,' she thought. '*What of my daughter? What will become of her? Will the two legs hurt her as well? Who will teach her the dangers of the world? Who will protect her now that I cannot?*'

The blackness began to close in around her. She could no longer see, but her unseeing eyes stared around her. She was so cold, so afraid. Her last breaths came in gasps from her lungs as her heart tried to beat in vain, and for one last moment her blind eyes stared franticly at the Gracies, at the creatures that had hunted her kind throughout the centuries, and she begged for help, her pleas unspoken yet so compelling. The last glimmers of life left her eyes as her breathing stopped and her heart gave one last feeble beat. A few twitches, and she was no more, her spirit departed to realms unknown, her flesh slowly cooling in the morning breeze.

All of them were weeping now as the fawn called urgently and fearfully, nosing her mother, who would never respond again to her touch. Crying in a soft voice, the fawn eventually turned toward Berwyn and nuzzled his hand again, trying to take solace in his presence. Not able to see for the tears in his eyes, Berwyn stroked the fawn, telling her silently she would be looked after and not to worry.

Rising on shaky legs, the Gracies and Demetrius stood silently for a while, until Reggie asked in a voice filled with raw emotion, 'Who did this and why?'

Huw spoke with a thick voice. 'The last Shadow, he was the one who shot her. I will find him and show him the wrath of life.'

Moving forward, Huw was stopped by Demetrius.

'No, he is mine,' said Demetrius in a dark and angry voice that was nearly a whisper. 'She answered my call, and she has paid for my arrogance. I did not anticipate when Eolus and the Vespre restrained the Wood Demons from driving you Gracies out of the forest, that their power to keep out others would be constrained as well. That is how your Shadow entered this forest.'

Silent for a moment, Demetrius spoke again, 'I can feel him running away to the north. He is no threat to you Gracies, and soon he will be a threat to no one or anything. He will be mine, and he will know my wrath as few have known it in the centuries uncounted. Well, my young friends, what will you do now? You are free to return to your homes.'

Huw said, 'No, Father. It seems right to call you that; does it not? We will come, and we will aid you in your mission to save the forests. There are none of us here who could forget what we have seen and felt here today. We will have to return to Platonia from time to time, as our families have need of us as well.'

'Thank you, my young friends,' said Demetrius. 'Come, let us find this foul creature who would slay mothers of the newborn. Then you shall see the power of Demetrius.'

Chapter Five

Rubicon

Daerahil rode his tired horse eastward, his legs and buttocks chafing against his worn, creaking saddle. Day after day Daerahil moved toward a destination forced upon him by a narcissistic father and malevolent first minister. As he rode the last miles upon the Haunted Road, he reflected upon his journey, pondering the inexplicable, irrational loss of his men on the road. After the initial disappearances, Daerahil had lost four additional men. This might have been statistically tolerable for troops riding in enemy territory, but here, in lands held by Eldora, it was completely unacceptable. There was no enemy here. No arrows sped from cover. No poisoned traps opened underfoot. Soldiers simply vanished.

No patrols could stop the losses either at night or during the day. There was no logic to the predation; men simply disappeared either at point or closest to the nightly campfire. The random nature of it was the most difficult thing for both Daerahil and his men to accept. Daerahil looked forward to reaching his post with stone fortifications offering protection for him and his men, rather than canvas tents and open ground. However, he knew in his heart that nothing tangible would stop this terrible unknown foe. Whoever hunted them would take his men and perhaps even Daerahil himself no matter the precautions taken.

Time and again during their journey from the Crossroads, Daerahil heard words in an alien tongue, sometimes barely audible, other times so loud and poignant he felt the breath of the speaker on his cheek. He spent hour after hour night and day extending his mental powers in search of this most elusive of foes. Always, he felt the presence of the creature that stalked them, but a warm trail soon grew cold; an artificial break in the trail leading to their hunter.

Daerahil knew then that whatever, whomever, hunted them had skill equal to or greater than his own, and that only if he kept his senses aware and searched all day and night would he find their invisible adversary. As a result, Daerahil teetered on the edge of exhausted collapse. He instinctively knew that the unknown assailant sensed his weakness, striking during Daerahil's fitful moments of sleep, or when his focus strayed. Daerahil suspected the real purpose of this drawn-out game was to defeat Daerahil's will; first to command and eventually to survive. Daerahil mentally vowed this would not happen; he would protect his men and eventually catch this most puissant hunter and bring him or it to bear at the end of a weapon.

Today he and his reduced company rode out of the last of the woods of Ackerlea into broken scrublands soon petering out to dust, sand, and broken stone. A high, thick overcast produced an unpleasant glare yet did little to alleviate the mood of gloom permeating the soldiers. Enormous stones, cracked and weathered, rose in jumbled heaps on their right to form the hills of the dark land. As they drew closer to the ancient ruins of the gates of the black land, Daerahil saw the dull glint of metal amongst the rocks, fused and melted in twisted shapes unknown in nature. Steadily the piles of ruined stone rose in height as the fortifications raised by Magnar during his terrible reign became clearer. Despite the incredible destruction, Daerahil saw the remnants of walls and watch towers appear before him. The last and greatest of these was a tower that reputedly had risen a hundred feet from a short steep hill. Now all that was left was an enormous pile of slag and broken stone perhaps thirty feet high; blackened streaks of rock snaked their way along the ruins and out toward the road before trailing away in the distance. Only the legendary Dark Lightning, a power unleashed and harnessed by Magnar, could have caused such destruction.

Magnar was the only known being in history born with the blood of all four races. This had given him the unique ability to use the elemental magic of all the races: earth from Men, fire from the Dwarves, air from the Greater Elves, and water from the Lesser Elves. According to history, Magnar had studied with the wisest men and women of each race, learning all they could teach him, before using that knowledge to commit unspeakable atrocities that resulted in his banishment from each race. Magnar then entered the Southern Highlands—now known as Plaga Erebus, the land of wounded darkness—a sparsely settled land where a unique hill, unremarkable in height or breadth, smoldered and muttered with sparks and flashes of a dark purple light. Seeing in this hill a power unknown in Nostraterra, Magnar somehow unleashed the energy trapped in the ground and created the Fountain of Hate. Dark Lightning erupted from this fountain, slaying the mortal servants of Magnar who had followed him into his exile.

Magnar slowly gained knowledge of this energy, knowing full well that if magic was expended, it must be replenished. The Dark Lightning waned as it expelled itself much more rapidly than its subterranean source could recharge itself. Magnar discovered that the life blood of sentient creatures could be fed into an aperture ten miles away from the fountain. The magic of life was perverted into the dark lightning, which destroyed all life that it came into contact with. As Magnar fed this most fell fountain, he learned to direct the lightning's course, raising a great temple complex over the aperture, the Sanguine Templar, the blood temple. As Magnar took control of the Dark Lightning, he used it to enhance his own magical abilities, while creating an impenetrable fence around the center of his land. Magnar's power attracted unscrupulous followers from the dark corners of Nostraterra. With his new allies—who quickly became little more than slaves—Magnar attacked and conquered the small villages and hamlets in the Southern Highlands. From there, his baleful influence spread grew until he dominated the warring tribes of Shardan and gathered legions of Dark Elves from the unexplored lands of far eastern Nostraterra.

At last he launched the war of conquest for which he had been preparing. All had gone well initially, until Aradia had escaped from the ruins of Phoenicia with the greatest Acies in Nostraterra. Using the crystals, she spied the one small gap in the protections of Magnar, and the group of heroes known to history as the Walkers had been sent through that gap to destroy the Fountain of Hate.

Daerahil recollected that somewhere on the road behind him was the spot where the Walkers had penetrated into Plaga Erebus. The exact location was unknown, destroyed in the ensuing conflagration that consumed much of Magnar's realm. But the knowledge that he had no doubt passed near or perhaps even over that same spot made the hairs on the back of his neck stand up. As a boy, he had imagined himself as one of the Walkers, those ancient heroes who had dared the embrace of Plaga Erebus. Now, so many years later, the reality, he decided, was not so romantic.

At last he and his men arrived at the entrance to the black land. Ruined heaps were all that were left where once formidable gates had stood. In their place were newly constructed, lightly fortified stone barracks located just outside the official border of Plaga Erebus. While Creon kept a garrison here, he steadily demolished the remaining original fortifications so that no one today could make use of the black land.

Daerahil was about to ride forward to officially take command of the garrison when an official messenger with an escort of three men arrived, galloping hard from behind on the road, their horses lathered in sweat and dirt.

'Messenger, why the hurry?' asked Daerahil.

The gaunt features of a man in his early forties stared blankly at him as Daerahil's men surrounded him and his escort, grabbing at the reins of horses whose riders had ridden them nearly to death. The faces of the escorting soldiers were also in a state of shock, but one old grizzled sergeant saluted Daerahil and said, 'Captain, I am Flibber, senior sergeant, now in command of the messenger's escort.'

'What happened to you and your men? Ten is the usual number of a messenger's escort.'

'We were ten when we left Titania,' Flibber said, 'but two nights ago we were attacked. Men vanished left and right around the campfire as something unseen took them into the darkness. Since daybreak, we have been riding as fast as we can, hunted all the way. This morning we risked our horses in one last dash for the safety of the garrison here. We abandoned supplies, only having some dried food and no water. May I take the men and the horses to the stables where they can be tended to?'

'You may, but what message is this man carrying?' asked Daerahil, pointing to the messenger, who now began screaming at the top of his lungs. This caused all of the soldiers to bare their weapons, but there was nothing to fight.

Riding forward, Flibber took the message tube from the crazed messenger's neck and handed it to Daerahil. Breaching the seals, Daerahil found a message addressed to him. Mergin informed him that the loss of so many men was another example of his incompetence. He would lose a month's pay for his failure, and any further loss of troops would be cause for greater punishment, including an extension of his exile in the Black Land. Shaking his head over his father's intransigence, for Mergin would not have dared send such a scathing letter without at least tacit approval, Daerahil did the only possible thing: ride to assume his new command.

Daerahil now formally relieved the garrison commander, Cirnir, and two hundred of the garrison's troops made leave to depart with the former commander. Daerahil had only brought one hundred troops with him, minus the losses on the road, but he knew that the discovery-and-excavation mission would arrive in six weeks with two hundred replacement troops, hardened cavalry veterans who had served for years in the deserts of Shardan, along with an engineering party. Now Cirnir and Daerahil rode to Cirnir's quarters so Daerahil could receive a formal brief before assuming his command.

Glancing at the narrow entrance into Plaga Erebus, Daerahil failed to prevent a shudder running up and down his spine. While Magnar was gone, remnants of his power lingered; his malice, while a pale shadow of its former self, still ran rampant throughout the land. The Temple ruins themselves were not a place Men would go willingly, and none had so far gotten closer than a league from the center of the ruins before being overcome with fear and horror.

There were rumors by the dozen about the Temple ruins and the road to the Fountain of Hate. Some soldiers claimed they had seen a darkened shadow flitting in and out of the rubble and ruin. No one paid the story much heed, until the first soldiers disappeared after the Great War. Here and there, a soldier vanished without trace, and the other soldiers grew nervous. It was always the same story: a soldier wandered off on his own, sometimes within a few hundred feet of his companions, and mysteriously went missing. No clues were ever left: no armor, no weapons, and not even any footprints. These were the stories that Daerahil heard from Cirnir over a cup of thin, bitter lager brought from Eldora.

'Just like the Haunted Road,' thought Daerahil. 'There is more to this than rumor, but what hunts us, I do not know.'

Wincing at the taste of the beer, Daerahil thought to himself that it had been improperly stored. But seeing the prince's slight grimace, Captain Cirnir said apologetically, 'I am sorry about the beer. It was good when it arrived. Food and drink tend to spoil faster here, and we know no cause for it. The fowl and livestock all die within a few days, so we must subsist on preserved or dried food during our stay.'

Daerahil responded, 'The remnants of Magnar, perhaps?'

'I do not know,' said Cirnir, 'but I am glad my tour is over.' He looked haggard, but he was not even thirty-one yet; Plaga Erebus had aged him terribly.

Daerahil knew that someone like Cirnir, whose speech and mannerisms betrayed a working-class background, could only expect promotion by volunteering for hardship posts, and there was no post considered more difficult than that of the garrison commander at Ianus Malus.

Cirnir said, 'I will soon return to Camden for an extended leave and rejoin the army in Shardan as a senior captain.'

'Congratulations, Cirnir, but you must be careful on the road home. I lost several men, and apparently the Messenger troop suffered severe losses on their way here.'

'Was that why that fellow was screaming?' asked Cirnir. 'He seemed out of his head, but your men hustled him away before I could inquire further.'

'That is no longer your concern,' Daerahil said. 'I will see to the man's welfare, never fear. You just be careful on the road home tomorrow. Now, is there anything else I should know about my new command?'

'Nothing good,' said Cirnir. 'My orders were to assist the engineers in the destruction of the fortifications of Magnar, but eleven men disappeared during my three-month stay. We never found any signs of them. You, too, need to be careful.'

There was nothing else to be discussed. Daerahil had the duty and fitness reports before him, and his orders were quite clear; he would lead a patrol through the northern fortifications and the Caves of Fear and return to await the arrival of the expedition. The Caves of Fear were a vile place still, with hundreds of Dark Elves' tunnels and dens carved into the mountainsides. Teams of engineers had searched these tunnels and found nothing there but the remnants of Dark Elves and the Men of Shardan and other lands.

Two days later, Daerahil ordered the men from the messenger patrol to return home, taking the afflicted man with them so that he could be treated by the Healers. Even now, the messenger did not seem to know who he was and had no sense of the present; his eyes stared at an unknown horizon, and occasionally he let out a bloodcurdling scream. He had no control of his bodily functions; his clothes had to be changed several times a day by soldiers, and he was fed and watered like an infant.

Upon receiving this order, Flibber said, 'With all due respect, Lord, there is nothing you can say or do to make us go back down that awful road. We will stay here.'

A shocked angry Daerahil ordered Flibber and his men to leave with Cirnir, but Flibber steadfastly refused.

'You may place us in shackles, my Lord, but we will stay here one way or another,' the man said.

Daerahil was now in a very unfamiliar situation. Never before in his years as a commander had his troops refused to follow orders. Worse, Flibber was not under his command but Mergin's, so, according to military law, Daerahil could do nothing. After thinking for several moments, he said, 'Very well, you may stay, but you are responsible for disobeying the king's orders.'

* * *

Daerahil and his new company rode out in the late morning light into Plaga Erebus and inspected the destruction of the Caves of Fear. Daerahil saw black holes in the hard rock of the hillsides stretching as far as the eye could see. Dark Elves, Trolls, and other foul creatures had dwelt here during the height of Magnar's reign. Daerahil extended his mental powers again, but despite the passing of centuries and the physical absence of the creatures, he felt only an overwhelming echo of angry terror. Unable to filter out these emotions, Daerahil temporarily ceased searching for the creature hunting them.

As they rode through the large valley, they occasional heard the rush of tumbling rock and the grinding of stones as engineers assigned to their three-month tour collapsed and demolished the tunnels one at a time. It was slow going and dangerous; while some tunnels had supports that could be removed, collapsing the tunnels, others had been hewn or blasted from the mountains and needed no support. While these were usually smaller tunnels, they were more numerous, so frequently the engineers were required to ascend the sides of the hills along the valley to pry loose stones and rock and sand from above, covering the tunnels below. Privately, Daerahil thought the whole exercise one of futility, but the king and the Council of Ministers thought otherwise.

Three days later, Daerahil took his first patrol out from Ianus Malus, going as far afield as his brief would allow, trying to regain his bearings and shrug off the oppressive weight of the black land. He and Hardacil led a patrol the next day toward Ackerlea. Seeing that a certain pile of stones had been moved, Daerahil bade his men ride back a little ways on the trail so that he might have some peace away from the black land. Hardacil and he proceeded alone until they came around a slag heap that was slowly being covered with bracken and weeds. Quietly, a messenger of the Lesser Elves slipped out from a nearby overhanging bush and brought Daerahil news.

Daerahil said nothing while the messenger relayed the tale of the Gracies and the incursions of the squatters who had drifted against their borders. Daerahil knew that the 'squatters,' in contrast to his father's classification as 'layabouts and wastrels' were mostly homeless veterans. They went into the hinterlands looking for land of their own, beholden to none. Now the thought that the very men Daerahil had commanded in the wars were being chased like cattle from their homes set a new fire ablaze within him. Picking up small rocks, he hurled them against the nearby boulders.

'What has my father said about the incompetence of our royal cousin Frederick in resettling these men and their families?' asked Daerahil.

'Nothing, but there is a rumor in Eldora that once your exile is over you may be sent north to put Amadeus in order. My Lord Ferox has said if the rumor is true, you should go to Amadeus. There, you will be away from the dangerous politics of the Citadel, and you will begin to rehabilitate yourself in your father's eye by fighting the corruption that Frederick can clearly not control.'

'I have no need to restore myself in my father's good graces,' said Daerahil defiantly. 'I have been punished for a crime I did not commit. Once my term of exile is up, I will return to Titania.'

'And then what will you do?' asked the Elf smoothly. 'Spend day after day, month after month, under Mergin's scrutiny, waiting for his treacherous mind to set another trap in which you will become ensnared?'

Daerahil felt anger welling up in him, but Hardacil suddenly reached across his horse to lay a hand upon Daerahil's shoulder. 'There may be advantages, Lord, in going north. Think of what might be possible to accomplish with these veterans that is still within the letter of the law. You could clean up the Princedom of Amadeus, all the while avoiding that vicious serpent; Mergin. Accomplishing these tasks would improve your standing in the king's eye and might lead to restoration of your military command much faster than a perpetual inspection tour.'

Contemplating for a few minutes, Daerahil said to the messenger, 'Does Prince Ferox have any influence through members of the Council to persuade my father and Mergin to send me north if I choose to want to go there?'

'A little, Lord, but your friend Zarthir and others who recently escaped arrest have more influence,' said the messenger.

'How did they escape?' asked Daerahil.

'I do not know all the details, Lord, nor do I know where they are hiding, but I can take a message to my prince and see if he has any luck in finding them,' replied the messenger.

Daerahil thought, 'Ferox almost certainly knows where Zarthir and his friends are hiding. I wonder what the real connection between them is and what they want from me.'

He spoke aloud, 'Please have Lord Ferox try and pass on a message to Zarthir that I will write shortly and leave here for you. You must go now—my men will be wondering what has become of me, and it would not do for us to be seen together.'

'You are correct, Lord,' said the Elf. 'I will return on the morrow for your message. We have left some supplies in an old chest and heavy leather satchels a furlong from here. Also, a gift of female companionship will be present here in one week's time, along with other Men who will aid your food supplies.'

Flushing slightly, Daerahil said, 'That would be most welcome. Thank Lord Ferox again for all of his aid.'

Saluting jauntily, the messenger turned his horse and, walking softly until he could safely canter out of earshot of Daerahil's men, departed.

'Well, this is some interesting news,' Daerahil said to Hardacil, 'but not another word until after the evening meal. Let us return to our guards and have them fetch the chest and satchels. Tell the men they are filled with books to explain their weight. Remember, we must keep our contact and aid from Ferox secret.'

Returning to Ianus Malus hours after they had departed, Daerahil and Hardacil went upstairs to the second level of the barracks to Daerahil's room. A few minutes later, several large men, huffing and puffing, entered, carrying two enormous travel-worn satchels, with a large locked chest as well. The men placed them down on the floor and withdrew, muttering that the prince must surely love to read, as these books weighed almost ten stone in each satchel and more in the chest.

Closing the door behind him, Hardacil helped the prince open the first satchel. Cunningly placed under some books and scrolls were carefully wrapped cheeses and fruits, cakes of the Elves, and other delicacies. Smiling for the first time in weeks, Daerahil opened the other chest, revealing two dozen bottles of wine and one dozen bottles of Spirits of Dorian, strong liquor made from the sugar reeds that grew along the banks of the Delta. While Daerahil preferred wine, he gratefully accepted this stronger addition, bidding Hardacil to fetch glasses.

The next morning, Daerahil silently cursed the headache that the Dorian spirits had left behind. Finishing a meager breakfast, Daerahil reflected on the nature of the upcoming expedition. The engineers were going to dare what no other Men had done so far: survey the ruins of the Temple Complex and begin preparations for removal of an active piece of the tower. Daerahil suspected his father also wanted to look for the Acies of Hiberius, presumably captured by Magnar after the successful siege of that Eldoran city by Magnar. There were other potential treasures in the rubble, and while they had little interest for his father, Daerahil knew, as did others, that almost all of the original Platina mined by the Dwarves had been stolen by Magnar; it was either in the ruins of the temple and its treasuries or within the accursed valley in some hidden place. Daerahil knew of the invaluable price of the metal, particularly that of wrought items. He therefore thought this might prove a new way to finance himself and his charities if any of the ancient hoards could be found.

Six days later, a messenger patrol from Eldora came to him with his first official news briefing since his arrival on the walls of Plaga Erebus. They apparently had no mishap on their journey, and when they asked about the previous messenger patrol, Daerahil supplied the barest outline of the disaster that had befallen them.

'I have orders to take them into custody and bring them back to Titania,' said the messenger.

'Do as you see fit,' Daerahil replied said with a shrug. 'Those men are not under my command. What news from Eldora?'

There was nothing new or relevant in the dry brief he received, but Daerahil asked, 'Is there anything else?'

'Well, Lord, just a caravan coming east on the Haunted Road,' said the messenger.

'Bound to where?' asked Daerahil.

'I do not know, my Lord, but I passed them by yesterday. They are probably only five leagues from here by now.'

'Thank you, you may go,' said Daerahil. Speaking to Hardacil, Daerahil asked, 'Is five leagues within my brief to send out patrols?'

Hardacil said, 'No, Lord, it's on the edge. Why not wait until tomorrow morning? They will come east, and you can then go west to meet them.'

'Yes, you are probably correct,' sighed Daerahil. 'Besides, there are few enough surprises, so I might as well wait until tomorrow to enjoy the ones that come along.'

* * *

The next day dawned gray and chilly, with a wind from the northwest and low clouds scudding across the mountains. It looked as if there would be rain by nightfall. Two saddled horses were brought to Daerahil and Hardacil, and an escort of twenty mounted soldiers with spare moutnts was soon ready to depart. Daerahil suspected that at least one or two of his sergeants were on Mergin's secret payroll, keeping a close eye on him. There might even be Shadows lurking about somewhere. When Daerahil had mentioned these thoughts quietly to Hardacil, Hardacil snorted and said, 'If there are any Shadows hereabouts, they are on the Ackerlea road, probably the only place that Mergin does not receive regular reports. By the time you traveled anywhere, my Lord Prince, your arrival would run before you all the way to the City. Only where there are few or no men of the City would Mergin need to set particular spies.'

Chuckling grimly, Daerahil said, 'You are probably correct.'

A few hours later, Daerahil saw the trade caravan coming along the road toward his patrol. Daerahil and his men rode forward to greet the caravan, a band of grim but peaceful looking traders with their guards.

'Hail, and well met,' said Daerahil. 'Few traders do we see east of the Elven encampment unless they are Dwarves in great haste. I am Daerahil, Captain of the King's fortress of Plaga Erebus. State your business and your destination.'

'Marnoth, my Lord, master trader,' said a slight hunched man in dull maroon robes covered in dust. Soft features with a large nose under dark brown curly hair, framed dark clever darting eyes; about forty or so. He gestured towards thirty equally dusty men astride horses leading nearly a hundred pack horses and dozens of spare mounts. 'These men are of my guild. We are bound to the great north eastern road, north of the black land, where we will trade our goods at Nexus.'

Daerahil knew that Nexus had evolved from the caravans and peoples moving well north of Plaga Erebus, connecting the Elves and Dwarves and Men to farther up the river with the Kozaki who lay along the north bank of the river and the men who dwelt in the great valley between the mountains of the Thumb and the Northern Forest, but below the great Cataract. Many different roads from all directions converged within a small but ancient village and well nigh half of all of the trade goods of Nostraterra passed through Nexus on their way to their final destination.

Most traders who traveled from Nexus to Eldora usually took the river west to Estellius, and then went north, south, or west, depending upon their destination. Those traders with financial means heading north invariably took the journey by river eastward that depended upon either favorable winds or expensive oarsmen. Frugal traders who wanted to avoid the expense or publicity of boats passed through the borderlands of eastern Eldora and western Kozak but still had to subject themselves to the customs inspections of Eldora. Only by using the Haunted Road between Plaga Erebus and the river could traders and others avoid the customs inspections and the curiosity of the border guards. While the realm of Ackerlea lay within the jurisdiction of Eldora, the Elves who patrolled the road on behalf of Eldora did not ask questions from merchants. Therefore it was unusual, but not unheard of, that well-equipped caravans would opt for the faster and more direct route through Ackerlea, avoiding inspection by the men of Eldora. This would generally shave off at least a week to ten days from their journey, but the Haunted Road kept all but the hardiest souls on the longer route.

'How and why are you using this road, when it is customary to use boats, or ride through Eldora and cross the Aphon well upstream?' asked Daerahil.

'Well, my Lord Captain,' replied Marnoth, 'our cargo is a bit fragile, and we stand to make a fair profit if we take the shorter, faster road east.'

'Cargo, is it?' asked Daerahil laconically. 'What sort of cargo could be precious enough to make you risk the Haunted Road?'

Seeing a few furtive looks and nervous glances from his fellow traders, Marnoth frowned. 'The rumors may lie thick on this road, my Lord, but there are few witnesses to support them.'

'Indeed,' replied an amused Daerahil. 'You and your men do not look terribly formidable, but perhaps I am only seeing what I am supposed to see. Again, your cargo?'

'Some coffee, my Lord, and some silks recently in fashion in Chilton, a few other odds and ends, nothing unusual,' said Marnoth, his sweating forehead betraying his fear.

'Then you won't mind if I take a look around, will you?' asked Daerahil. 'No contraband in your goods?'

'No, Lord,' said Marnoth woodenly. 'Examine what you like.'

Poking and prodding at the nearest bale, Daerahil thought there was something not quite right here. Few men would risk the road despite the profits, and rarely in such a large party with so many horses. Gesturing to his soldiers to aid him, he told them to carefully inspect the cargo sacks. Sure enough, there was a great quantity of unroasted coffee and some fine silks. Wine there was, too, and hidden amongst the coffee beans were very rare hams and pungent yet delicate cheeses.

'So this is what you would not have me find?' asked Daerahil, holding aloft a mustard-cured ham of South Shardan and a wheel of exquisite cheese.

'Yes, Lord, that is it, we feared they might be confiscated.' replied Marnoth too quickly, blotting his forehead on his dirty sleeve.

'I see they do not bear the seal of the border guards. Well, well, some of these items must be seized indeed,' said Daerahil, 'along with some of your coffee. Our supplies have run low.'

Seeing the relief in the man's face, Daerahil knew he had not yet found the real reason behind the traders' choice to take this road, but knowing he was close to the truth, he desired to extend the game slightly. Bidding his soldiers to mount up, he had the ham, the wheel of cheese, and twenty-five pounds of unroasted Shardic coffee placed on some of their spare horses.

'Well, Marnoth,' said Daerahil, 'I believe that we can overlook these infractions and let you ride on your way.'

'Thank you, my Lord,' replied Marnoth. 'I do not know how these goods could have been un-customed by the border guards.'

'Peace, merchant,' said Daerahil. 'I am not part of the border guards. So long as you bring something back this way equally rare and tasty, there shall be no trouble.'

'Thank you, Lord,' said Marnoth. 'I will surely find something at Nexus for you.'

'Well and good,' replied Daerahil, 'Now let us ride together since we are going the same way, and you can tell me of your journey.'

As the miles slowly wore away, Marnoth began to relax more and told his tale slowly about the journey from the Crossroads, where he had picked up this cargo. His men and his horses were based there and rode between the Crossroads and the Nexus, usually through Eldora but occasionally through Ackerlea if the profit was worth the risk. Smiling at the clear lie, Daerahil said nothing until his soldiers had ridden nearly a furlong ahead, anxious to be free of the dust and smell of the caravan.

Quietly, with his eyes facing front, Daerahil said, 'You, sir, are a liar. Four of your horses have Stone Burrs in their tails. I spent enough time in the deep desert to know them when I see them.'

Seeing the alarm in the man's eye, Daerahil saw him lean forward unconsciously and for the first time saw the dusty pouch on the man's saddle tied in front of the leather seat. It blended with the brown dust of his horse and but for the trader's slight body movement, Daerahil would never have seen it.

'Now, my good trader, you can slowly and carefully hand me that small pouch on your saddle, or I shall set my sword tip at your throat and my soldiers and I will tear your cargo apart and place you and your men under arrest,' said Daerahil.

A man across from Marnoth swiftly began to reach under his cloak, when Hardacil threw a small dagger concealed in his sleeve into the man's chest. Gasping slightly, the man quickly slumped over his saddle. The poisoned dagger worked quickly, the life ebbing from him in just a few moments.

'This is the last time, trader, that I shall warn you,' said Daerahil. 'Hand over the pouch to me or you will join your most unfortunate friend and never reach your destination.'

Glancing around him, Marnoth tried to take reassurance that he and his men outnumbered the Prince and his guards three to two, but there was no guarantee that even if these were all the soldiers that the Prince had with him, there were not more ahead. Besides, attacking a Prince of Eldora was madness even if he was in disfavor.

'Please, Lord, this pouch is nothing, have the rest of the hams and cheese if you like,' said Marnoth desperately.

Raising his left hand to make a whistle with his fingers, Daerahil was about to signal when Marnoth hissed, 'Very well, Lord, I will argue with you no longer, here is the pouch.'

Daerahil guessed at its contents before he opened it. Seeing his guards were still disinterestedly astride their horses in a steady walk, and that the traders were not anxious to make more trouble after seeing their chief soldier killed in his saddle, Daerahil reached down and poured the contents in his hand. Small silk purses with a hard center filled his hand and, opening one of them, Daerahil saw a beautiful blue white diamond, the size of a quail's egg, flash and glitter in the sun. Holding it up to the light briefly, Daerahil knew that these were diamonds desperately smuggled out of Shardan, thought to provide financing for the insurrection. Indeed, Daerahil knew that the Shardic diamonds were legendary. Only six or seven per year were legitimately exported from Shardan; they were the single most valuable commodity in the world, even more so than Platina or the Fire Opals of the Dwarves. Brilliant in their clarity, they had a blue white hue found in no other stones in Nostraterra. Additionally, they were rarely smaller then a quail's egg, making them truly spectacular to behold. One of them was worth at least fifty thousand gold pieces, and the fifty he held in his hand were probably worth more than the entire Duchy of Camden and all its inhabitants. The diamond mines were under strict scrutiny by the guards of Eldora, as many years ago, a diamond was found for sale in the City that was not accounted for in the official customs tally.

Mergin, then in the infancy of his career, had been outraged, declaring that these diamonds would not be allowed to finance the rebels or bring home any undeclared profits to Shardan. From that day forward, the diamonds were the most regulated trade in Eldora. To possess a stone without a clear claim of its origin and pathway to Eldora meant death, usually by torture. Only three other illegal stones had been found in the realm, and their owners and the merchants involved had been swiftly punished. The last had been over ten years ago, and Mergin and the Council thought they had stopped the trade in illicit diamonds once and for all. Now it was clear that the diamonds were leaving Shardan, but not coming to Eldora. They were going north, furthering the war and killing more of Daerahil's men.

His face mottling with rage, he was about to call to his guards when he noticed the person directly in front of Marnoth lower their hood and glanced back at him.

'Larissa,' he said with a surprise. 'What are you doing here of all places and with these traders engaged in such treasonous activity?'

'Well met, my Lord. There is much to tell. Will you not hear me out before you summon the rest of your men?' said Larissa, her red mane streaming out from its hiding place.

Thinking about this for a few moments, Daerahil replied darkly, 'Yes, very well, I will hear you, but I will hold the diamonds until you are done speaking, and unless you are very persuasive, you and these men will be imprisoned and tried for aiding the very insurrection that costs so many soldiers of Eldora their lives. It seems once again I have you at a disadvantage, but I would take back my words about your beauty fading at our last encounter.'

'Thank you, Lord, for your forbearance and your apology,' said Larissa. 'Marnoth why don't you continue on ahead,' she said. 'The Prince and I will follow just behind you.' She led her horse out of the column, waiting for the rest of the merchants to pass, and only Daerahil and Hardacil remained with her. Daerahil gestured for Hardacil to ride a few horse lengths behind him, as he rode side by side with Larissa.

'Now, what about these diamonds? Why do you profit from the death of my soldiers?'

'While it is tragic that men of Eldora are killed by rebels, they would be killed regardless of the diamonds,' Larissa answered. 'The rebels are actually divided into two factions. The first is made up of mindless thugs and criminals, brigands both noble and common who grow fat on the miseries of war. The second and smaller faction is comprised of men who view themselves as patriots, wanting to free their land of a foreign occupation, but willing to treat with Eldora fairly and honestly once the occupation is over. It is this faction, Lord, that is able to exercise some restraint on those Shardans who would butcher every man and woman of the west and north that they could touch, both abroad and here in Eldora. Without this restraint, the slaughter of innocents in addition to attacks on soldiers would overwhelm everyone, forcing your father to lay waste to all Shardan, weakening the army to the point where kingdoms farther east and more savage would descend upon the western lands.

Society and culture in the west as we know it would cease for decades, perhaps centuries, as the mindless hordes in eastern Hagar and Azhar would savage the fertile lands of the west. It is to prevent this greater tragedy for all men on both sides of this conflict that these diamonds are sold. Stopping the money from the sale of the diamonds would not reduce the loss of the Men of Eldora and Kozak but to the contrary provoke a conflagration that will consume us all. Only a change in policy toward Shardan will actually allow the rebellion to come to a natural, peaceful end and allow the soldiers to come home. Lord Zarthir and your other monied friends have only been involved in Shardan since you were no longer on the frontier. They only want the same things that you do: peace, the veterans brought home to their families, their welfare looked after, free trade with Shardan. What can be wrong in this?'

'What is wrong,' said an indignant Daerahil, 'is the fact that you, Zarthir, and these restrained rebels are profiting from the deaths of hundreds of soldiers every year, a hideous practice that must be stopped.'

'The death of soldiers must be stopped,' agreed Larissa, 'but that can only happen once the war is over and the allied troops are withdrawn from Shardan. Peace can be just as patriotic as war, and my Lord Zarthir is quite patriotic, but disagrees with your father on the current state of affairs in Shardan, as you might well suspect.'

'How can aiding the insurrection be considered patriotic?' asked Daerahil in a very dangerous but quiet voice. 'Where is your loyalty?'

'What if I told you, Lord, there is loyalty to Eldora and Kozak and there is loyalty to your father and his policies, and they are not necessarily the same thing?'

Pausing for a moment, Daerahil thought about all the events that had occurred recently and said, 'There is truth in what you say, but say on before I pass judgment, as this does not seem relevant to your actions.'

'Lord, the occupation of Shardan is foolish and a waste of good men, good money, and good resources. As you have said publicly, the Shardan people can either be annihilated, abandoned, or pacified and as they have chosen not to be pacified, then they can either be annihilated or left to their own devices. What if they are left to their own ways?' asked Larissa. 'Many of the more educated and moderate rebel leaders are warm to an alliance both political and financial with Eldora so long as they are allowed to govern themselves internally. They would make peace with Eldora and acknowledge the Overlordship of the King.'

'Well and good,' said Daerahil harshly. 'This is what we have tried to accomplish all along. Misguided though my father's policies are, the security of Eldora cannot be overlooked. Let us return to the diamonds.'

'By trading in diamonds, these moderate rebels in Shardan receive money to finance and control the rebellion, with some profits going to Zarthir and his friends so they can continue to court influence that will allow you, hopefully, to become King. When the time comes, Zarthir, his many friends, and others will support you in a claim for the Kingship.'

'My father is King last time I checked,' replied Daerahil dryly. 'And barring an unforeseeable accident, he will rule for at least another hundred years, if not longer due to his Elven blood. My brother and I are not so lucky, and it is indeed possible that the next generation of our family, my future children or my brother's, will rule the kingdom instead of us. Regardless, my brother is next in line, so what you say has no merit.'

'If circumstances were different, Lord, if your father became ill, would you not prefer the Kingship over your brother?' pressed Larissa.

'Of course I would, as my brother is as much to blame for my exile as my father and that treacherous Mergin. More importantly, since I have arrived here he has done little to aid me and nothing to detract from my misery. Someday he and I may resolve our differences, at least so I hope, but it shall be on my terms, not his. However, you have said nothing that would tell me how and why I might become King someday, and if this is all that you have, I shall proceed with an arrest, which along with the diamonds may allow me to leave here sooner rather than later.'

'Then there is little that I can say, Lord. You must call your soldiers.' Pausing for a moment as Daerahil studied her face with a frustrated expression, Larissa said, 'Oh yes, there is one last piece of news. Did you hear your brother has a new lady friend?'

'No, I did not,' said a bewildered Daerahil. 'What is it to me?'

'Probably not much, Lord, just that you know her,' said Larissa.

'What? One of the distant cousins of Kelsea or the daughter of the Duke of Camden? My brother will be forced into a loveless marriage soon enough with one of those schemers,' said Daerahil. 'Little joy will he have in the union of the Kingdom and a politically suitable match.'

'No, Lord, her name is Findalas. Perhaps you have heard of her?'

'Findalas' said an incredulous Daerahil. 'That little slip of a commoner who is a healer?'

'The very same, Lord, the very same,' said Larissa.

'My father approves of this match?' demanded Daerahil. 'No, you are trying to trick me. My father would never countenance such a relationship, even in private. You must be mad.'

'No, Lord, the truth is well known. She was brought to the Citadel two weeks ago for the feast commemorating the fall of Magnar. Many tongues were set wagging, but she was greeted warmly by your father and sat at the high table,' said Larissa.

Stunned, Daerahil did not know what to say. The rage and anger towards his father became palpable. 'How dare he allow my brother his woman, while mine was ripped from me and condemned to a fate worse than death!'

'I believe, Lord, your father said that a true woman of Eldora was superior to any Shardic or even Kozaki woman, especially a common whore.'

'When did he say this?' whispered Daerahil.

'At the end of the feast, Lord, when a minister politely asked after Findalas' lineage,' replied Larissa.

'He embarrasses me again in public. Is not my humiliation enough for him?' asked Daerahil in a voice thick with rage.

'Well, Lord, this was the same day that Lord Mergin had a portion of his manhood removed by one of the healers. Apparently your kick was more accurate than you imagined, and your father was apoplectic that Mergin should suffer such an indignity,' said Larissa.

Daerahil was pleased that Mergin continued to suffer as he did, but now his father's mood would be even blacker towards him. Not even the diamonds would secure his return to power before his time in exile was over. Still, the thought rankled deeply, and he would come back to the diamonds in a moment.

Shaking his head wearily and with disgust, Daerahil said, 'I do not know what to say, Larissa. What of my brother? How is he enjoying his newfound friend?'

'With great vigour, Lord,' said Larissa. 'There is talk that he will petition to the King to endow Findalas with a small title for her aid in caring for him and his patrol. This would allow Findalas to be considered of noble blood even if only by a lawyer's trick.'

The purple of anger gave way to the white of disbelief and rage in Daerahil's face. In a small voice utterly devoid of feeling, he said, 'Now I see the point of your tale. This way my brother gets the Kingdom, the woman that he loves, and I remain stuck in the wilderness.'

'Yes, Lord, your brother even suggested that to aid you in your return to society, the Duchess of Camden would make a fine wife for you and that your father should insist upon this as a condition of your return.'

Roaring, Daerahil said, 'That is unconscionable! He knows how much I can't stand the woman.' Daerahil thought briefly of the portly, pasty woman from Camden whose father was duke of that small realm. Considered eligible due to the fact that she was the only child and heir to the fortune of the entire Duchy, her looks and her vile demeanor had conspired to keep her single since she came of age. Hearing the shrill rasping tongue in his head and thinking about those squinting watery eyes, Daerahil thought he might throw up.

'So, now both of them are conspiring against me?' asked Daerahil.

'I think your brother has only your best interests at heart and that the Duchess would restore you to good odor at court and keep you from any other missteps,' said Larissa with a strange glint in her eye. 'There is one other thing, Lord, that you should know before you decide to arrest me and my men.'

'What is that?' asked Daerahil.

'Immediately prior to your trial, you received a small note from Hala, did you not?' asked Larissa.

'Yes, though clearly someone else wrote it for her, as all I was able to do was teach her to sign her name,' replied Daerahil with some surprise.

'Was the note genuine, Lord?'

'Yes, Larissa, it had the secret marks that I taught her to place on the paper that look innocent but tell me that it was from her. Besides, the note had her scent upon it, a very expensive and unique perfume that I had made from a perfumer in the City. Why do you ask?'

'I have another note from her Lord, one that was delivered by our friends from Hala while she was with the patrol heading into South Eldora.' said Larissa.

'What? I thought that she was dead!" exclaimed Daerahil in stunned disbelief, 'I sent her a poison so that she could end her life with some form of dignity and spare herself the pain of her torment.'

'Here is her note, Lord. Why not read it for yourself?'

Daerahil saw that the wax seal was undisturbed and that the letter was contained within a thick traveling canvas. Breaking the seal, he was immediately ensconced within the perfumes of Hala. Tears of sadness and longing began to course down his face as he read.

'*My dearest prince, I hope you are well. I am now the whore for these men, but as you know, I can please a man above all others, so there is one guard sergeant that has taken me to be his woman for the rest of the journey. I do this to survive, not for me, but for our child that I carry within me. This was the great news that I hinted at in my last note to you, but I could not bring you this news after the trial. I will bear you a son or a daughter in the following months, and the gods willing it will be a healthy baby. I will not be allowed to return from Shardan; I only hope that you can come and see me and our baby someday. I will wait for you until then, lord, and I will do whatever I must to survive. Do not be overlong, I cry each night for you and wish to hold you again. Farewell beloved,*

Hala.'

Daerahil slumped in the saddle. 'Everywhere I turn, I lose someone I care about. I am forced into exile, and now I will be told to marry that insufferable cow if I want to return to Eldora with full honors. Plus, I will never see Hala again, nor will I ever see my child. Is this not so, Larissa?'

'Yes, Lord, it is,' she replied.

Muttering darkly, Daerahil dismounted and, leaving Hardacil to keep an eye on Larissa, his black mood overwhelmed him and he was left alone with his bitter thoughts. Many minutes passed as he paced aimlessly, trying to see a way out of this new prison. The Duchess would never accept a political marriage, insisting he be faithful to their miserable marriage bed. One trip to the joy houses for him, and she would hound him till his death. Plus, Hala would face a life of destitution and depravity, alive only at the whim of whatever man would pay for her in Shardan. Bearing and raising a half Eldoran child would make her life much more difficult, and it was unlikely that she and the child could survive.

A small voice then spoke in the back of his mind. *'What if you were King? Then you could marry Hala and take care of Mergin and his foul friends forever. Your brother could be given Ammadeus and sent away. Frederic is useless and weak, no loss to the Kingdom if you made him Duke of some Shardan province.'*

Acknowledging this feeling ripened a dormant seed deep within the recesses of his mind. A great lust for power and revenge fueled his heart as he replayed the events over and over in his mind. He called Hardacil over to hear his counsel.

Hardacil supported Larissa's viewpoint. 'You continue to suffer from the outrages and insults of both the King and Mergin, and now even your brother. The only way for you to ever have peace and more importantly the woman you love in your lifetime is to seek the Kingship. Clearly Zarthir is your only means to power in the kingdom. If you refuse, you will be shunted from one undesirable position to another. Even if you marry that wretched pig of a woman, the Duchess of Camden, you will never be trusted by your father and Mergin again, no matter how innocent you are in the plot that nearly killed your brother. Hala will be left to rot in Shardan, your child forced into prostitution or worse to survive. You must side with Zarthir and allow Larissa to take the diamonds for sale, but you must insist on tribute, my Lord, or you will be a conspirator without independent means.'

Daerahil then bade Hardacil return to guard Larissa as he thought through all of this new information. Nearly an hour passed before he returned his attention to Larissa. A decision made of both logic and rage now focused his will utterly on the ultimate goal: the displacement of his father as King and the subjugation of his brother.

'I believe that you Hardacil and Larissa are correct,' he said. 'I have little choice. Only by removing my father from power one way or another will I ever be able to achieve the peace and greatness for which so many in Eldora and Shardan have suffered and died in vain. Only by assuming the kingship myself will I recover my beloved Hala and lead my life the way that I see fit. Larissa, you mentioned the support of Zarthir if the Kingship ever came into question. What exactly did you mean?'

'First, Lord, you will overlook the diamonds now that you know they will be sold to indirectly aid you in your quest to become king. Minister Zarthir and his friends, along with several members of the King's Council, and others outside Eldora, regard you as a man of vision. If something unforeseen happened to your father, an unexpected illness, perhaps, then you would have to support your brother as king. With support from the army, Zarthir and his friends, his Shardic allies, and the support of others I have referred to, you would have little trouble supplanting your brother as King. You know you are more popular amongst both the army and much of the populace, my Lord,' said Larissa with an appealing look in her eye.

'That is true, but this is all happenstance and nonsense. My father is healthy as a horse, better protected than any man in Nostraterra, and my brother still wields the majority of the nobles and the Council. I do not know what you aim to accomplish by dangling a great prize in front of me that can never be obtained,' said Daerahil with both anger and frustration.

'Do not say never, Lord, for even now there are forces that are moving to aid you in your quest. The only thing we need to know from you is if you will continue to support Minister Zarthir as your friend and ally when and if the time comes,' said Larissa.

'What does this support entail?' asked Daerahil.

'Well, we think that it would be quite poetic if you were to countenance Minister Zarthir's marriage to the Duchess of Camden in your stead, Lord. This would give Zarthir the protection of nobility and legitimize his place in the realm from mere merchant Prince and Minister to an actual Duke in waiting.'

'Done,' said Daerahil. 'If ever I have that power, then the next Duke of Camden shall he be. Is their aught more that Zarthir requires?'

'Not him, Lord, but there are others who will have similar requests for personal recognition. Trade would have to be protected and structured throughout the realms. The war would have to end, the troops be brought back home. There may be one or two other minor conditions that others may want,' said Larissa.

'Who are 'they'?' asked Daerahil. 'You keep saying 'we,' and I get the feeling you mean others outside of Eldora.'

'Perhaps, Lord, but I am not at liberty to say, and the time is not yet ripe,' said Larissa. 'Besides, I do not know the particulars—only Zarthir does. Perhaps you could meet him once your time in Plaga Erebus is up.'

'Certainly, but why does he not come to me now?' asked Daerahil.

'Lord Daerahil,' chuckled Larissa, 'the only way I escaped the Shadows and was able to come see you is that no one knows of me yet. Zarthir is in hiding, his mobility is strictly limited, and he can communicate with the rest of the world only through a few intermediaries such as myself.'

'Allow me to search your mind Larissa, I must know if you tell the truth.'

Larissa's face blanched white, a line of sweat along her brow, as she said in a quavering voice, 'Please lord, believe what I say, last time you entered my mind was horrible, worse than having my body forced to compel!'

'Peace Larissa, I will be gentle and brief, if you do not resist, you will feel no pain at all.'

Too terrified to speak, she nodded her assent. Daerahil gently entered her mind and softly probed for falsehoods, but all he found was her desire to convince him rather than lie to him, buried under fear and tension. Withdrawing gently, Daerahil patted her hand and Larissa's wild eyes slowly began to calm down. Once she had regained her composure, he said,

'I will allow you to take the diamonds and continue on to Nexus,' said Daerahil. 'You will express my support to Zarthir and the others who will stand by me when and if the time comes. However, you will bring to me ten percent of the profit of your transactions as my tribute and shall invest it for me quietly, discretely, and without a whisper returning to Mergin's ear, do I make myself clear?'

Fuming inwardly that this would cut half of her profit as well as the rest of the caravan, Larissa knew she had little choice. Besides the fact that they could not fight their way through. Zarthir said the true leader of this conspiracy had been quite clear that Daerahil must be seduced, not antagonized. While Larisssa suspected that there was no true leader other than Zarthir, she had no evidence to contradict him.

'You drive a hard bargain, my Lord, but it shall be so.'

Extending his hand, Daerahil said, 'Give me one of those stones to commemorate our bargain. I will wear it secretly as a token of the hope that I shall get to wear it openly soon.' Grimacing, Larissa did as she was asked.

'Is there anything else, my Lord?' she asked through clenched teeth.

'Yes,' said Daerahil. 'Take some of my profits from this transaction and make certain that monies reach either Hala herself or whichever man is sponsoring her. While my child will be born in Shardan, he or she must survive with my beloved Hala. If my family dies, then my motivation to aid Zarthir will be substantially reduced.'

Sighing out loud, as this was another specific matter that would require her personal attention, Larissa replied, 'Very well, my lord, I will see to this personally, but I cannot guarantee that she will survive.'

'There are no guarantees in life, Larissa, but your word that you will do all that you can is good enough for me.' Climbing astride his horse again, Daerahil was silent for a few moments before regaining his more even frame of mind. 'Well, this has been a profitable day for you and me,' he said. 'My soldiers and I shall escort you to Ianus Malus today and northwards on your journey tomorrow. This way you should clear the Haunted Road without mishap, and your goods shall be more secure. Let us now talk about the different ways that Zarthir and I can help one another.'

Riding alongside each other, Larissa and Daerahil began to relax and even to renew some of the mutual affection and warmth that they had felt for each other years ago. As they caught up with the soldiers, Larissa asked provocatively, 'Do you have a private bath chamber that we might use when we get to Iannus Malus? I am quite dirty from travel.'

'Yes, indeed, Larissa, and I will join you if I may,' said Daerahil. Now he knew who was to be his female companion as promised by the Elf messenger, and smiled at the though.

'You may, my lord. It has been far too long since we have enjoyed each other's company.'

As they neared their destination, Larissa thought that despite the risks and danger of arrest, Daerahil was now part of Zarthir's plan, and, after tonight,

Larissa knew that Daerahil would be persuaded even more to participate in days to come.

Chapter Six

Vagwar

Two weeks after his meeting with Larissa, Daerahil rose early. Striding to the window, he saw what could only be the dust of the new patrol arriving, escorting the team of excavators to their new project. He dreaded the morning security report. Five of the men who had arrived at Plaga Erebus with him had since vanished, officially deserting but unofficially disappearing without a trace.

Daerahil used his mental powers constantly to search for the man or creature hunting them, but all of his efforts were fruitless. Too many men with too many thoughts provided background interference, but it was the psychic horror of Plaga Erebus that overwhelmed him each and every time he opened the channels of power in his mind. If he had a specific person upon which to focus his powers, such as his friend Hardacil, who Daerahil heard climbing the stairs, he could push distractions out of his mind. But without that focus, even his mighty brain was overwhelmed, and all that he achieved was a terrible headache. Too many people had died horribly here, their souls somehow leaving a psychic stain so powerful that Daerahil could not mentally penetrate. Constantly angry and frustrated, Daerahil did his best to temper his feelings, but slowly the futility of his position overwhelmed the skilled tactician within, until by now he had begun to lose his self-control, even flying out in impotent rage from time to time.

Hardacil entered after a brief knock and without waiting for a reply. 'Lord,' he said, 'the new team of excavators, engineers, and surveyors has arrived with another supply train. There are separate horses that I suspect contain more special rations, but, Lord, please try to contain your drinking.'

'Very well, I will try. In the meantime have my breakfast sent up. I wish to eat alone. I will be down presently.'

Daerahil descended the stairs from his quarters, observing three hundred men arriving in the compound. Two hundred excavators, surveyors and engineers, led by a senior engineering captain, and one hundred extra guardsmen, led by a senior lieutenant once under Daerahil's command on the eastern frontier. Starting in surprise, the lieutenant returned Daerahil's salute with crisp alacrity. Casually replying to the salute, Daerahil approached him, saying, 'Troand, it is good to see you after all this time.'

'Yes, Lord Prince, I well remember the day when you rode away to the city. I have not seen you since.'

'It's only been two years, actually,' said Daerahil. 'When I left, you were a lowly sergeant. You must have done well to be promoted a level per year. What are your orders?'

'We will rest here for two days, allowing the engineers to familiarize themselves with the techniques used to build the caves. Captain Ralard commands the engineers, but I command the expedition, subject to your supervision. I have orders from the king himself.'

Daerahil turned to the engineering captain. Barely twenty-two, he was pale with anxiety at meeting a former prince of the realm and a living legend amongst the regular army.

Sensing the anxiety from this mediocre man, Daerahil knew he could vent some of his pent-up frustration upon a toady who must be in Mergin's good graces to be appointed to a command at such an unusually young age. However, he took pity on the man, who maintained a salute for several minutes before Daerahil returned one half-heartedly.

'Captain,' said Daerahil laconically, 'you may see to your men. Troand will apprise me of your daily status.'

'Yes, Captain, thank you,' said Ralard, who departed with his men after another crisp salute.

Troand then handed Daerahil a sealed messenger tube with both ends embossed with the purple sealing wax used by the king for official messages before sending his men away from the prince and his friend.

'Why do your excavators want to see these lesser caves?' asked Daerahil. 'They have been inspected closely for goods or treasure before this.'

'The Mining and Building Corps has spent decades formulating new theories and ideas about how to bring a vibrant piece of the accursed temple out of the ruins, to study it at their leisure,' said Troand. 'They hope that by understanding the magic that courses through the stone constructions here, they can understand the dark magic in its entirety. You are aware of the great reward the king has posted for the first man or men to bring back a piece of the temple still imbued with magic?'

'Yes, I am aware of the reward,' said Daerahil, 'as well as the terrible price that all who have attempted to do so have suffered for their failure.'

Any piece of the tower previously pried or broken loose from the tower ruins discharged Dark Lightning, slaying the handlers and then becoming nothing more than an inert chunk of rock with metal imbedded within its structure. The magic that had coursed through Plaga Erebus during Magnar's terrible reign was gone from them, the inner workings of metal fused into incomprehensibility. Only a piece of the Temple, with the elaborate, ornate gossamer-thin strands of metal intact, with magic still coursing through their fibrous threads, was worth anything to the Alchemists of Eldora. So far, every attempt to remove a piece of this most unique stone work had failed, the magic fading as it lashed out and killed all those nearby.

Daerahil said, 'I think the Mining and Building Corps will have to throw the scrolls away, both old and new, when they see what they are up against. I have never seen such metals and stones worked together.'

'Well, Lord, their success is not my problem. Ralard is the one who has to report his findings, not I. I only have to make sure they return safely to Eldora before I am transferred to my next guard detail, constructing a new bridge over the Aphon near the Delta. If they are successful here, then I will enjoy sharing their reward, but if they fail, my career should not suffer too greatly. Now, with your permission, I must see to the bivouac of my men.'

'Well and good,' said Daerahil. 'Come see me in my rooms when you are done.'

Later that night, Troand sat and quietly enjoyed Daerahil's 'extra rations' as they were now called by Hardacil and a select few who were in Daerahil's favor.

Speaking aloud, Daerahil said, 'I see I am to escort you to the ruins and back with half my garrison. Is there anything else?'

'No, Lord, only your protection. The rumors of what happened to you on the Haunted Road along with your losses here have come to my attention.'

'Indeed, Troand, there is something or someone who hunts us at will. None of my defensive plans have safeguarded my men. I will do my best to protect everyone who journeys to the temple ruins, but if this creature comes for any of us, I fear there is little I can do. Is there any other official business or can we relax and drink without concern for duty?'

'No, lord, we can just enjoy this quiet time. But first let me return this wine to the ground. I will be back in a moment.'

Troand lurched up from his chair and descended the stairs, a bit unsteady with wine and spirits of Dorian. He headed toward the closest latrine. Entering, he ignored the strong stench of urine and feces that filled such a structure, intending to empty himself and return to Daerahil's quarters for more drinking. Breathing a sigh of relief, he spouted a stream into the trench and, finishing, turned toward the washbasin to wash his hands, when he saw a figure cloaked and hooded. Not having heard the man enter the latrine, Troand threw up a sloppy salute before he felt an overwhelming fear permeate him. His bladder released a last few drops as the hooded figure suddenly moved toward him. All Troand saw as his life faded were piercing blue eyes filled with madness.

* * *

Daerahil spoke with Hardacil about Daerahil's political situation while Troand was gone to the latrine for several minutes, but then Daerahil felt a tiny yet piquant mental intrusion into his mind, the fading fear of a dying man accompanied by a dark presence unfelt since the Haunted Road. Springing up, Daerahil said, 'Hardacil, place the entire barracks on alert and bring ten of our best men to the latrine immediately.'

Daerahil and Hardacil descended the stairs, with Daerahil retreating into the very center of the parade ground outside the barracks complex, where he could see anything or anyone come at him. Hardacil's voice could be heard ringing throughout the stone walls and buildings, and only a minute later came the tramp of booted feet at the double-quick march as Hardacil returned with the required men.

'To the latrine!' said Daerahil.

Thinking their captain more drunk than usual—for despite Daerahil's best efforts, his men knew that somehow he possessed a great supply of alcohol—the men ran with Daerahil toward the latrine. The first men entered and cried out a warning. Daerahil pushed ahead and saw Troand's clothes neatly hanging from the wooden wall in a gross parody of a man's form, with an unknown rune written in blood on the ceiling.

'Search the barracks and out-buildings,' Daerahil ordered. 'Troand may still be alive but injured.'

The men moved to follow his orders, but they and Daerahil both knew that Troand was gone, never to be seen again.

Daerahil had the guards doubled around his quarters for all the good it would do and drank himself into a stupor, hoping that if the creature came for him, his end would be swift and painless.

Arising the next morning, he assumed Troand's duties and escorted the engineers just inside the official borders of the Plaga Erebus. That day and for several more days, the surveyors spent their time examining the Caves of Fear, trying to add more knowledge to that of their predecessors of the mining and building skills involved, and moreover the magical techniques, of Plaga Erebus.

When the allotted time ended, they reported to Ralard that there was little left for them to learn. Bare rock only told so much, and they were ready to depart for the Sanguine Templar.

The next day dawned clear for Plaga Erebus. The ash clouds from the fuming broken remnants of the Fountain of Hate were blown away by the upper wind from Ianus Malus, and the men had a clear view of a most inhospitable land indeed. While the ruined volcanic pit was content to only exude streams of blue sparks and lightning and smoke and a fine ash that needed to be swept away at this distance, the closer one got, the worse the ash fall. Battalions of prisoners from the Shardan campaigns were forced to clear the roads monthly between Ianus Malus and the ruins of the Sanguine Templar and back. Their overseers were men of Eldora who were hardened criminals who had been offered the choice to oversee war prisoners for a ninety percent reduction in their sentence. Initially many of these convicts were happy when presented with this opportunity, but for most of them, happiness faded to hopelessness within a few weeks, to a bleak horror soon afterwards. Nearly all of the overseers went mad eventually, running screaming into the night, forever lost in the deserts of this terrible land. Sometimes these unfortunate men were seen running hither and yonder across the plains of Merrikh, quickly dying in the vast desert. Some said these men were the basis for the rumors of a shadowy creature that preyed upon Men, but Daerahil thought this nonsense. '*No*,' thought Daerahil, '*the shadowy creature is something different, akin to, or the same as, that which hunted us on the Haunted Road. Not mythical Werewolves not crazed Men, perhaps an ancient creature of Magnar that survived his fall.*'

David N. Pauly

A month ago he would have snorted aloud, disdaining the thought that some sorcerous creature had been hiding and living for hundreds of years in the most inhospitable land known to man instead of leaving and preying upon lands far richer. The memory of the soldier's head spinning slowly from the tall tree on the Haunted Road reminded him that behind all great mysteries there is a simple truth.

Two days after they left the northern hills, they came to the outskirts of the temple. The blackened walls lay for half a mile in diameter, ornate structures combined with low black walls, with hints of a deep red color splashed haphazardly upon them. At the center of this complex was the squat ziggurat that anchored the oppressive darkness that remained in this dreadful land. Thousands had been sacrificed atop the blood pyramid, their life force feeding the Fountain of Hate, replenishing the energy expelled as streams and bolts of Dark Lightning. Even from a distance the psionic reverberations from the excruciations of those slaughtered during the Age of Torments assailed Daerahil's perceptive mind, and he was forced to turn his mind inward completely. While Daerahil knew that he would be less effective in sensing the minds of his men, much less hunting for the creature, he had no choice but to insulate his thoughts from the psychic scream of terror and despair that perpetually radiated from the Temple complex.

Once they arrived at the site, Daerahil dismounted from his horse and had a couch and a small tent set up for his comfort, with the opening facing toward the ruins of the Temple. Hundreds of years after the fall of its master, it still had a brooding malevolence, an evil feel that would not go away. It was hoped that by slowly dismantling the Temple and placing the pieces on wagons and sending them south through Plaga Erebus to the borders of Shardan that the sunlight would be able to break the remnant of their unholy power. The undertaking would be vast; thousands upon thousands of tons of stone and metal would have to be carted away before any sizable progress could be made.

First, however, it would be necessary to determine how to defeat the magic that coursed through much of its structure. This magic could not be seen, only felt as one got close enough for the hairs on the back of one's neck to stand on their own. Metal close enough to the walls would begin to sparkle and snap, as the Dark Lightning found a conduit in which to travel. Holding the metal in one's bare hands was an invitation to death, as the magic would build rapidly, instantaneously flowing through the metal into one's body. The only way to

129

discharge a section of the walls was to find a break in the stone where the metal threads were exposed and then connect these threads to a copper spike driven into the ground.

The problem was the metal strands were so small and dark they blended into the rock. One could not see the threads until they began to spark and glimmer: too late if one was holding any metal. The only safe way was to use a dense wooden pole with copper at its tip and see when and where the arcing of the magic began. The pole had to be at least twenty feet long to keep the holder safe, and certain alchemical powders must be used in the varnish of the pole, or the Dark Lightning could and would still course along its length, slaying the bearer. Any break in the powder coating spelled disaster, so the pole could not rub against the sharp edges of the stone. Each gap had to be explored extremely carefully. Finally, the cost of such poles was exorbitant, and the engineers only had so many of them, and if the poles were lost, the men would have no way to determine whether the stones were alive or not. Even when a small section of wall was determined to still be full of magic, Daerahil knew of no way to remove the stone with the magic intact. This thankfully was not his problem, but that of the engineers.

As the day wore on, Daerahil became bored, and three days of the same routine had Daerahil mounting his horse and riding with Hardacil around the ruins, hoping to see something interesting or at least different. There was a sharp slag heap adjacent to the ruins; standing close to the tower, but outside the perimeter, it was almost two hundred feet high and offered an encompassing view of the ruins. Daerahil had been quite a rock climber in his youth, and now, seeing a clear vantage point, he quickly became excited, even if it was a trivial challenge.

Calling for ropes and metal spikes, he changed into flexible clothing and soft rope-soled shoes. Daerahil was able to find a purchase and slowly climbed a small split in the rock, like smoke up a chimney. Reaching the first level about thirty feet from the ground; Daerahil saw the slope of the stone become a little easier. Drinking some water from his pack, he began coursing back and forth, slowly making progress. Hardacil shouted for an update, forced to remain on his horse with an ankle he had twisted the night before stumbling for the latrine after too many glasses of bitter beer.

'I am fine,' replied Daerahil. 'Another hour should see me to the top.'

Just under an hour later, Daerahil stood atop the slag hill, the ruins of the Temple spreading before him. He could see the surveyors and excavators forming a loose circle around the temple remnants, mapping and diagramming the outer wall. The plains of Merrikh stretched to the south, a vast and desolate land pockmarked with the holes from rocks hurled from the fountain during its destruction. Nothing grew there; the fetid dust choked any living things trying to establish a toehold; only the sands and ash were plentiful upon that ghastly plain. Around the remnants of the temple lay only the stony hills of the finger of rock upon which the Sanguine Templar had been built. Thrusting out from the Tarin Mountains, the stony peninsula had the same look as the stones of the temple, but unlike the temple stones, the natural rock could be touched safely with bare hands and worked with normal tools.

Daerahil knew that plants and trees were slowly working their way up the distant faces of the outer mountains and hillsides of this land, but it would be many generations before they could be called green. Here in the heart of the ancient realm of evil, it was difficult to remember trees and running water, fresh air wafting through flowered gardens. Only death and decay were present, a foul staleness that robbed the tongue of moisture, the heart of laughter, the mind of hope.

Looking about him again, Daerahil realized that dusk would fall in an hour or so. He made ready to descend from the hill and saw a small shadow flitting at the edge of his vision. Turning, he saw a moving shape, dark and quick, moving through the edges of the ruins. Suddenly it approached a surveyor, and then, without a sound, the man disappeared.

Crying down to Hardacil that there was a problem on the northwest side of the ruins, Daerahil quickly descended the hill to the ground below. His horse had been brought up, and he galloped around the rude pathway through the dust and ash that had been cleared by the feet of others. Arriving at the place where the man had been, Daerahil could not proceed until his protective leathers were brought to him. Silently cursing his lack of focus in climbing the hill rather than patiently waiting with his men, Daerahil had to wait as others went amongst the stones. They returned with a cloak that had blood on it, but there was no trace of the man who had been wearing it.

Fanning out, they conducted their search until full dark threatened them. They then returned to the encampment along the road. 'Right before my eyes he went,' muttered Daerahil.

'You keep saying that, my Lord, but do not blame yourself,' said Hardacil. 'But for your vision up on the hill, the man would have disappeared without a trace. Now at least we know there is indeed someone or something responsible for these disappearances.'

'Yes, we know that,' said Daerahil. 'But who or what are they? Why would they take these men?'

'I do not know,' said Hardacil. 'Perhaps you will learn more tomorrow.'

'Double the guards tonight, and bring our pickets in close to the camp. I want no further casualties,' said Daerahil.

The next morning, however, they realized that one of the guards had gone missing: the man on the farthest edge of the encampment. After searching fruitlessly until near luncheon, Daerahil ordered the men back into the ruins.

Nothing did they find that day, nothing but dust and flies, small black flies that somehow gleamed in the oppressive permanent twilight of this land. Biting and stinging, they appeared without warning, distracting the men from their search. Daerahil had heard of these flies: it was said that death preceded and followed their appearance. As evening drew to a close, Daerahil gratefully suspended the excavation mission for the day and called his men back to camp.

The night slowly deepened to full blackness. Suddenly a voice muttered loudly in his right ear, echoing through the camp: the same voice Daerahil had last heard upon the Haunted Road. He jumped to his feet and demanded that more wood be thrown on the fire and torches be lit. The men looked at him strangely: it appeared that only Daerahil and Hardacil had heard the spectral words. Waking early the next day, Daerahil had his men report and found that none had disappeared during the night.

Heartened by this success, Hardacil asked, 'Lord, what was different about last night that none of the men disappeared?'

'I do not know,' whispered Daerahil. 'Have a rumor spread that I brought an ancient book of alchemical spells to chant for our protection. It will reassure the men.'

Swiftly this lie permeated the camp, and the men took heart. Daerahil slowly and steadily contracted the survey mission so that the men were not susceptible to attack.

The next few days were uneventful, and Daerahil began to believe they might have found a solution. Until, suddenly, there came a cry from the man posted on top of the slag hill. This time, Daerahil and his cavalry were there in moments.

It didn't seem possible that anyone could have gotten through their perimeter, but right in front of them, just inside the ruins, a young surveyor's crumpled form was found. When they turned his body over, they saw that his throat had been torn out. Yet there was very little blood on the ground.

'May the Gods save us; we have a *moreserce*, a blood drinker, amongst us.' muttered one of the men. Daerahil was shocked, but things now seemed to be adding up. Only a blood drinker, one of the mythical horrors of the Great War, was rumored to kill like this, draining a body of its blood. Daerahil thought for several moments, trying to remember the proper name from the dark speech of Magnar. Then he had it: *Vagwar*, the living dead.

They had been deemed a myth for centuries. No *Vagwar* had ever been seen, killed, or captured, yet still the rumors existed. Now it seemed there was again one amongst the living.

Making a decision, Daerahil moved the men out of the ruins and back to their camp the next morning, ordering a full rest day to give the engineers time to formulate a plan to excavate a block of stone. He took the opportunity to ride toward the slag hill, taking only Hardacil. Hardacil's ankle was still too sore for him to climb, and so Daerahil ascended alone. At the top, he dismissed the guards, wanting to be alone for a little while.

Below him, Daerahil saw his guards dispersed around the hill. Gazing around the ruins, he saw the excavators working in tight-knit groups. All seemed to be going well. With a sigh, he leaned back upon the ground and rested his head against a boulder.

Brooding about what could be done to rectify this current mess, he never heard or felt the shape approach, only saw it reach for him out of the corner of his eye. Rolling before the shape could grab his throat, Daerahil nonetheless found that the shape had hold of him. A cold skeletal hand clamped down over his face, muting his cries for help. Through cold fingers obscuring his sight, all Daerahil could see was a dark figure grappling with him, its form hidden by a swirling black cloak that seemed to move like smoke. The world around him turned gray. Daerahil seemed to see his father's face before him. He heard his father's voice naming him a fool and a failure, a disgrace to his land and his legacy.

'Well, Father, perhaps you are right,' thought Daerahil. 'I was fool enough to follow your orders and come to this place of ancient holocaust. Still, I wish you were here dying with me, so that the realm might be saved from you.'

Daerahil's mind then drifted back to more poignant memories. He saw again the face of Hala the night he had told her that he loved her. He remembered fishing with his brother when they were young children; the first large trout coming into Daerahil's basket, when nothing seemed more important. The hiss of sand against his cloak on that cold desert morning when he rode out to the cheers of his men for his first day of command. Months later slumping against the saddle of his horse, driving off the last of the rebels in his first actual battle. The fragrance of Shardan coffee, the spices of a fine, yet simple, desert meal. Rich wine from Chilton; the salted breeze from the bay of Dorian on a moonlit night. All these images the Shape drew from Daerahil's mind, and now, willingly, his spirit began to detach itself from his flesh, bowing before the inevitable onslaught of a superior will.

Then Daerahil recalled the slain children of Cratan, a Shardan village pacified by Shadows and the Iron Brigade, a particularly brutal company of soldiers that executed the king's will absolutely. The broken faces of veterans returning home to poverty and despair, no future in the brave new world that was the king's vision for them. Corruption and waste, carnage and despair: these were the works of the king's policies. Now, even fading with his last thoughts, they kindled a rage deep in his heart greater than any he had felt before.

Forcing his mind to extend itself to its full potential, despite the terrible presence of the pain of the dead, Daerahil mustered this newfound strength. He lifted a feeble hand, and, jostling the hand of the Shape over his heart, Daerahil felt the necromantic connection falter. That brief moment allowed him to ascend from the pit of hopelessness he had descended into and lock his will with his opponent's. Silently, for what seemed like hours, but was in actuality only moments, the two struggled. Daerahil was able to return to a conscious state and, seeing the shape clearly again, broke the hand free from his neck.

Struggling to free himself, Daerahil let out one oath that called the attention of the guards. But they were twenty minutes away at the fastest climb; Daerahil knew he must deal with this adversary on his own. Hissing in a strange speech that hovered on the edge of comprehension, the figure came at him, flowing as quick and deadly as a tide overtaking people caught in mud flats. This time, Daerahil was aware of his danger and used his powers to deflect the mental strike to his emotions and his mind more easily. Daerahil thought of his dagger, but the attacker was too mobile; if Daerahil concentrated on a physical defense, he could not focus on his mental battle. Suddenly Daerahil recognized the language being spoken, or rather hissed, as the Dark Speech, the language created by Magnar and used only during his terrible reign. Few knew that tongue today, but Daerahil was one of them, intensely curious about the language created and spoken by the most powerful entity in the history of Nostraterra. Yet he had never heard the language spoken until now. Recalling a few words, Daerahil shouted out, 'Stop, cease this attack!'

Pausing, the figure hissed at him, 'How do you know my speech, little one? You will be a curious meal.'

'No, wait,' said Daerahil, as more words of the language returned to his frantic mind. 'My men are on their way up. You will not be able to escape from us again. Why do you attack us?'

Hissing in rage, the entity said, 'You are food to me. You are the backbone of this group. With you dead, they will run helpless back to the structures at the entrance of this land; I will have several of them in their retreat.'

'Surely there is something else that you can eat besides the blood of Men?'

'No, the blood of Men, Dwarves, and especially those hateful Elves is what sustains me in this land,' the creature said. 'I will feed on you and someday emerge to consume those who left me here to die.' It moved to attack again, clawed fingers raised to strike Daerahil's eyes.

Daerahil knew his life was measured in seconds, and he played his last desperate card. Feeling the revulsion within him, but knowing that he must survive today to act for tomorrow, he said, 'Stop; and I will send you some prisoners from the labor gangs. That way you will not risk being caught.'

Pausing, the creature said, 'How do I know you will keep your word?'

'How do I know, *Vagwar*'—using the creature's ancient name—'that you will not attack me and my men tonight?'

Chuckling with insane glee, the Vagwar said, 'Very well, perhaps there is more to you than meets the eye. I will wait for seven days, but you must bring me five men. Do not expect to see them again. Meet me on the north side of the temple ruins with the men during the night. If you do not come, you will not leave this land alive. You will not be able to retreat to the walls of this land without my taking you personally, my young scholar.'

With that, the shadowy shape flitted to the edge of the hill and vanished into the gloom of the land. The soldiers were just now coming to the top of the hill. Circling the prince, they were in high praise that he had driven off the shape. Crumpling to the ground, exhausted, Daerahil found that he was much more tired than he should have been after such a brief contest. He realized his will to resist and his very soul had been attacked, and that any other man, without his mental powers, would have succumbed, left drained in every respect upon that bleak hill.

After a while, he had the strength to descend to the waiting guards and refused to answer any questions. The guards that had come to his rescue had astonishment on their faces and dread in their hearts, for they had seen Daerahil falter and swoon at the feet of his demonic adversary. Yet while he had not slain the vile thing, he had somehow driven it off, and that gave the men hope that it was not all-powerful. Cheering their prince loudly, they helped him into his saddle and escorted him back to the encampment. There the healer gave Daerahil a restorative potion, allowing him to regain a portion of his strength. Posting the guards even more closely, Daerahil dozed until the evening meal was ready. After dinner, he told Hardacil, 'I will need five of the labor prisoners, preferably the weakest ones you can find.'

'There was a gang of them just going through here earlier today,' said Hardacil. 'Why do you need them?'

'Please, old friend, ask no questions. Simply bring them to me within the next few days. I have a special plan for them.'

Seven days later, five men from the labor battalion stood before him, and, as the day drew to a close, Daerahil casually suggested that the laborers be placed closest to the ruins on the left side of the encampment that night to give warning if the Vagwar returned. Daerahil had the juice of several medicinal herbs added to their evening food, so they were soon befuddled and docile. Earlier, Daerahil had whispered to Hardacil that the two of them were going to take the labor prisoners out that night to the far side of the temple. He added that Hardacil should not act surprised at anything he saw or heard.

Hardacil was perplexed, but he would follow his prince to his death willingly, so he asked no questions.

Sleeping until two hours past midnight, Daerahil awoke and, shaking Hardacil awake, casually walked out from the sleeping soldiers, telling the two outermost guards on perimeter duty that he Hardacil would take over watching the prisoners. 'Move closer to the fires and sleep. Hardacil will wake you at dawn so you can renew your vigil.'

Gratefully the men acquiesced, happy to place themselves as far from the outside of the circle of danger as possible. Believing they were free from prying eyes, Daerahil had the labor prisoners up on their feet tied to a rope cof-fle. Daerahil had withdrawn the sentries earlier that day, so there was no one watching them.

After a quarter mile, Daerahil murmured to Hardacil and they both lit the torches they had brought. 'We will take the prisoners as bait and see if we can flush out the Vagwar,' he said to Hardacil.

Taking two of the torches, Daerahil and Hardacil began riding around the ru-ins of the temple complex with the men walking in front of them. The prisoners were too stupefied to know they were in the most immediate danger.

Arriving around the north side of the temple, Daerahil and Hardacil bound the feet of the prisoners and forced them to sit upon the ground. The wait-ing became nearly unbearable as Daerahil confronted his own fears that the Vagwar would come for all of them and not honor the bargain they had made. Just when he thought he could stand no more and was about to return the prisoners to the camp, the Vagwar came, flitting up and down the men in the coffle, skeletal hands flashing, its face and form still obscured by its shadowy cloak in the flickering torchlight.

'You have brought me the dregs of your kind,' it whispered now in the com-mon tongue. 'They will not satisfy me for long.'

'Our agreement remains nonetheless,' said Daerahil with far more confidence than he felt. 'These were least useful to me and my king, and thus the least likely to be missed.'

'I will honor our bargain, but you must leave this land and never return in seven days.'

'I cannot leave,' said Daerahil. 'I am here for six more weeks. If I leave before then, I shall be imprisoned or worse by the king. You will have to slay me if you can, but I will smite you if I may.'

Hardacil drew his sword at that point, prepared to attack this fell creature, but waited for a sign from his prince before acting.

Laughing darkly, the Vagwar said, 'Well met. You have courage in addition to your unique mental powers and language skills. Perhaps leaving you alive would be more amusing than killing you now. Tell me, what do you know of me?'

'You are a Vagwar, in the tongue of the Black Land. A *Moreserce*, one of the living dead: a blood drinker of the ancient world. Your kind has always existed in rumor and myth, though none of you have ever been seen before.'

Laughing again, the Vagwar said, 'Little fool, you know nothing of me or my kind. Once, there were several of us going forth to do Magnar's bidding, forcing lesser beings to bend to his will. All but I were slain in the Great War. Moreover you are incorrect. Many have seen me, but they are no longer amongst the living.' Laughing again, the Vagwar asked, 'Why did you make this bargain with me, young prince? Your bravery runs before you even in this land.'

Startled, Daerahil asked, 'How could you know anything about me?'

'You know little of anything beyond your mortal ken, but answer my question before I grow angry,' said the Vagwar.

'I will answer your question, but let me see your face' said Daerahil.

'None except those who are dead have seen my face since the fall of the Temple. Would you join them?'

'You will show me your face, or you must try to kill me. You may succeed, but I will hurt you before I go.'

Flitting and grasping Hardacil's throat with one hand, the Vagwar struck Hardacil's sword from him with other. 'Perhaps I will kill this one instead of you and slay him before your eyes before you renounce your words and bow before me.'

'Slay my friend if you can, but I will slay you in turn,' said Daerahil. With that statement, he pulled a bow from beneath his cloak and, drawing it to its full, said, 'The arrow before you is a remnant of the Greater Elves of Phoenicia, made perhaps by Emedius himself. It will slay you if you harm my friend.'

Releasing Hardacil, the Vagwar swooped suddenly toward Daerahil and looked at the curiously wrought arrowhead in the dim torchlight and laughed again. 'No, little one, it was not made by Emedius. It was wrought indeed by a Lord of the Elves, but your knowledge fails you now. Kaitan, son of Phaidros, had a son, Kaibur, and he it was who wrought this arrowhead. Or perhaps I did. It is difficult to tell in this poor light.'

'You,' said Daerahil, the arrow point wavering from its target. 'How could you have wrought this arrow?'

'That is another story for another time. Perhaps someday you will know it in full. You are brave, and while you may miss with that accursed arrow, you might not, and I have no desire to be weakened by such a wound. Crown Prince of Eldora, I will show you my face, and I will tell you a little of my story, and then we can continue our tale before I feed on your fellows.'

With that statement, the Vagwar pulled aside his hood and stood before Daerahil. Black was his hair, with streaks of gray. His face was one of ruined beauty, with dark blue eyes staring from pale skin, whiter than snow. The eyes were sunk deep into the skull, and the mouth was thinly lipped, with four sharp teeth protruding slightly from the lips.

'Verily, a Vagwar I am now,' said the creature, 'but once I was one of the most powerful of all the Greater Elves. I stood by the side of Aradia and her uncle and helped them make the Crystal Towers that kept our lands safe for millennia, the greatest achievement of skill that mattered in Nostraterra. Long ago that life was taken from me by Magnar. I was abandoned by my kind, left for dead, though many who survived the great siege here on this plain knew I lived. I stand before you now as a Vagwar, but once I was honored throughout the land of the Greater Elves. They along with all others shall pay for their treachery. I have tested your bravery from our first encounter on the Haunted Road, as you call it, until now, when I ordered you to leave. You are braver than any of your kind I have found over the centuries and my knowledge and powers will aid both of us. I can aid you in your quest to be King of Eldora, but I have my price.'

'What can you do for me, and why should I trust you?' asked Daerahil.

'You should not trust me, or anyone else in this world,' said the Vagwar. 'I do not know yet how I shall aid you. I must assess your strengths beyond your bravery and your relative intelligence. In time, as I see your merits and test your mettle, I will aid you greatly. There is no one else who can make you such an offer, so think well before you discard the opportunity fate has brought you.'

'Your offer is as unholy and foul as you are,' said Daerahil. 'I want nothing from you but safe passage from this land for me and my men.'

'How do you know my offer is unholy?' said the Vagwar with sly humor and a condescending smile. 'You haven't heard anything about it. Do not lie to me, child, when you say you want nothing from me. Do you not yet hunger for revenge upon those who have hurt you? Are you content to return to your land as an example crushed beneath the heel of your father's minister? Would you give up your dreams of changing the very nature and structure of Nostraterra simply because you find me distasteful?'

'How do you know of any of this?' demanded Daerahil.

'You are not in a position to ask questions, mortal child. You intrigue me, however, and you may be the person that I have been looking for since the Sanguine Templar fell. Come, let us make this bargain. I will take these Men you have brought me, and I will attack no more of your fellows while you are in this land. I will fast for you as my pledge of good faith, but you must have more Men for me once your time in this land is done. Tell your men that you rode out and challenged me in single combat and drove me off. That will increase your stature and give you the excuse you need to explain the loss of these laborers.'

'My men may not believe I defeated you so easily a second time,' said Daerahil.

Suddenly striking out with both hands, the Vagwar drew deep gouges with his fingers across the chest of a surprised Hardacil and scratched his nails across Daerahil's throat.

'Do not argue with me again. Do we have an agreement, or shall I consume you two as well?'

-The End of Book Three-**Myths**-

Dear reader,

We hope you enjoyed reading *Myths*. Please take a moment to leave a review, even if it's a short one. Your opinion is important to us.

Discover more books by David N. Pauly at https://www.nextchapter.pub/authors/david-pauly-fantasy-author.

Want to know when one of our books is free or discounted for Kindle? Join the newsletter at http://eepurl.com/bqqB3H.

Best regards,
David N. Pauly and the Next Chapter Team

You might also like:
Cradle of the Gods by Thomas Quinn Miller

To read the first chapter for free, head to:
https://www.nextchapter.pub/books/cradle-of-the-gods-epic-fantasy-adventure

About the Author

Hailing from suburban Chicago, David Pauly attended the same high school where they filmed the 80's classics, Ferris Bueller's Day Off, 16 Candles, and the Breakfast Club. College at UW-Madison was awesome, where David majored in History, minored in beer drinking, and enjoyed his first taste of freedom. Working for a year after graduation for Domino's Pizza convinced, David that law school was preferable to food service so off to Washington and Lee he went.

Another graduation brought yet another re-location, this time to sunny New Mexico. Practicing law in the Land of Enchantment, David spent several years building up his practice, but always felt that something was missing. While David loved the turquoise skies and spicy food, he was looking for something more.

A life change prompted David to take a sabbatical from practicing law, and move to Paris, where he obtained a certificate in cuisine and pastry, from Le Cordon Bleu in 2003. Unable to find work, David left the wonderful magic of Paris behind, returning home to New Mexico, to revive his law practice, and care for his five rescue dogs. Single for the first time in 10 years, David took refuge in re-reading his favourite Fantasy and Sci/Fi books, returning to his childhood refuge, distracting him from a mundane depressing existence.

Voraciously re-reading books like Lord of the Rings, The Chronicles of Narnia, and Dune, The Martian Chronicles, and the Foundation Trilogy, David always wondered what would have happened after these stories ended. So, one snowy night he let his imagination run free and began typing a few sentences of what would eventually become an epic fantasy novel. Ten years later after countless re-writes and edits, begging family and friends to re-read it all, David published his first novel, The Fourth Age Shadow Wars.

Currently busy with his law practice, and precocious 6 year old daughter, David writes the sequel to Shadow Wars, Dark Shaman when he has time. Dreaming of having more time to write and cook, David soon hopes to put away his legal shingle for good, never having to answer the most frequent question asked by his clients "Am I going to Jail again?" with the response, "Yes, yes you are."

Lightning Source UK Ltd.
Milton Keynes UK
UKHW011907120221
378724UK00008B/463/J